Miss Drake Investigates

A Jazz Age Mystery

Stephen E. Stanley

Stonefield Publishing

I could not, at any age, be content to take my place by the fireside and simply look on. Life was meant to be lived. Curiousity must be kept alive. One must never, for whatever reason, turn his back on life.

ELEANOR ROOSEVELT

Contents

Books by Stephen E Stanley

A MIDCOAST MURDER
A Jesse Ashworth Mystery

MURDER IN THE CHOIR ROOM
A Jesse Ashworth Mystery

THE BIG BOYS DETECTIVE AGENCY
A Jesse Ashworth Mystery

MUDER ON MT. ROYAL
A Jesse Ashworth Mystery

COASTAL MAINE COOKING
The Jesses Ashworth Cook Book

JIG SAW ISLAND
A novel of Maine

DEAD SANTA!
A Jesses Ashworth Mystery

MURDER AT THE WINDSOR CLUB
A Jeremy Dance Mystery

UP IN FLAMES

A Jeremy Dance Mystery

ALL THE WAY DEAD
A Luke Littlefield Mystery

CRUING FOR MURDER
A Jesse Ashworth Mystery

A GRAVE LOCASTION
A Luke Littlefield Mystery

POTTERY AND POETS
A Luke Littlefield Mystery

MUDER AND MISBEHAVIOR
A Jeremy Dance Mystery

A PRAYER IN ORDENARY ATIME
A Novel of the Home front

TRAILER TRASH
A Jesse Ashworth Mystery

WIND IN THE SAILS
A Jeremy Dance Mystery

MURDER ON SHAKER HILL
A Luke Littlefield Mystery

DEATH INSURANCE
A Jeremy Dance Mystery

A PRAYER IN TIME OF WAR
A novel of the home front.
ROAD KILL
A Luke Littlefield Mystery

MISSING
A Jesse Ashworth Mystery

A PRAYER IN THE DARK OF NIGHT
A novel of the Home Front

HAWAIIAN HOLIDAY
A Jesse Ashworth Mystery

DEATH IN A TIN CAN
A Luke Littlefield Mystery

Chapter 1

Isadora Drake stood in front of the mirror adjusting her clothe hat. She spun around to see the fringes on her dress move and shimmer and was pleased with what she saw. "Not bad for an old maid of twenty-one," she said to herself. The pale green dress, she thought, was the perfect complement to her red hair and fair skin.

"You look like a flapper," said her grandmother Rose as she walked by Isadora's room.

"Better a flapper than a floozy, Granny," Isadora countered.

"I don't know about that," commented Rose. Since her parents' death in the flu epidemic of 1919, Isadora, who had barely survived herself, and her brother Peter had lived with their grandmother. Peter was now an engineer at Edison's Menlo Park. Their grandmother Rose had been a music hall singer in her younger days and knew all about being a floozy. "You be careful at the dance, Izzy. You know what men are."

"Men are many things, Granny. But it's just a dance." Isabel kissed her grandmother on the cheek and headed out to her new 1922 Oldsmobile. She was grateful for the electric starter and didn't miss the old hand cranked model T at all. She shifted the car into gear and pulled out of the driveway and headed off to pick up her friend Anna Greyson.

Anna was waiting on her parents' front porch as Isadora pulled up to the curb. "Let's go," yelled Isadora, "before all the good men are taken."

"You think there are any good men around?" asked Anna as she climbed up into the passenger seat.

"Doubtful, but we'll see." The two left the town and continued through West Bath until they pulled up at the New Meadows Inn. The inn, built in the 1890s, next to the New Meadows River, was a Victorian resort built for the more affluent visitors.

"Now begins the adventure," whispered Anna as they watched a car full of young men head into the Inn.

"Let's just hope they are good dancers. I don't need some goon stepping on my new shoes."

"Hopefully one or two of them will have a flask on them," added Anna.

They showed their invitations to the tuxedoed waiter and entered the large public room. The mirrored ball in the middle of the high ceiling was sending glimmering points of light throughout the room. A large seafood buffet had been set up and the band was playing a foxtrot.

"Let's grab some food and scope out the area," suggested Anna.

"Not a bad idea at all," agreed Izzy. The two young ladies walked along the buffet filling their plates and then headed off to one of the tables that circled the dance floor.

"Oh, look there's Billy Brown," she said as she waved him over. They had both known Billy Brown since first grade, and he was what they considered a pal.

"I should have known you two heart breakers would be here."

"I'm surprised you're here," said Isadora. "You don't dance."

"I'm here to people watch." Billy replied.

"Well, I'm sure it's not the female people you're here to watch," Isadora shot back.

"Don't be a bitch, Izzy," Billy responded.

"Well, I never!" said Isadora fanning herself pretending to be shocked.

"You never? No one would believe that." Billie opened his jacket to reveal a silver flask.

"Alcohol? I'm shocked!" Isadora took the flask that Billy passed to her and took a swig. She then passed it to Anna. "Not bad."

"My father got it from Canada," Billy admitted.

"Your father," said Anna, "has good taste."

"Look what just walked in," Billy whispered as the three of them watched a young man with blond hair swagger in.

"Ronald Anthony Wicker," Isadora almost spit out the name.

"Yes, and don't ever forget to use all three names," added Anna.

"Wouldn't dream of it," said Isadora.

Ronald Anthony Wicker spotted the three of them at the table and headed over.

"Oh, crap," whispered Isadora. "He's seen us."

"Good to see that the lower classes of Bath are represented tonight," said Ronald to the three of them.

"Yes," said Billy, "I'm glad they invited you."

"I'm surprised you're not hanging out in the men's rest room." Ronald shot back.

"Why are you looking?" asked Billy.

"Funny guy," Ronald responded. "Maybe I'll save a dance for you ladies later."

"Don't put yourself out," said Anna. Ronald waved at them and headed over to another table.

"What an ass!" said Isadora as they watched him greet a table of young ladies.

"I see I'm not the only one to have a flask." They watched as Wicker took a flask out of his pocket and passed it around the table. One of the girls dropped it, bent over to pick it up and wipe off the neck of the flask and passed it back to him.

"Those Brunswick girls are no better than they should be," said Anna.

"I never understood what that means," said Billy.

"It means," said Isadora, "that the likely hood

that there are virgins at that table is very much in question."

"Virginity is overrated," replied Anna.

"Speaking of virgins," said Billy. "Mary Brockton just walked in."

"Is she carrying her Bible?" Isadora sniffed.

"That woman is headed to a nunnery," added Anna.

"The last time I talked to her," said Billy, "she bragged to me that she was the most religious person in town."

"No argument from me," Isadora responded.

"She's always running off to mass," said Anna

"I wonder why they call it that?" asked Billy.

"Beats me," said Isadora. "I'm a Congregationalist."

"No kidding," said Billy. "The three of us met in Sunday school if you remember."

"And Mrs. Wilson's first grade," added Anna.

"Those were the days," sighed Billy. "Looks like the dance floor is getting crowded. Which one of you wants to dance with me first?"

"You can't dance," said Anna.

"I've had lessons. I can do a mean fox trot."

"In that case," said Isadora, "I'll give you a try."

True enough Billy and Isadora glided over the dance floor light on their feet. "Someone's had lessons for sure," commented Isadora.

"My father insisted upon it. He said I'd never attract a wife if I couldn't dance."

"Are you looking for a wife?" asked Isadora, but she knew already the answer to that question.

"I don't think that's in the cards for me, but no sense in telling the old man that."

The music stopped and the two headed back to their seats. "Where's that flask?" asked Anna when they returned to the table. Billy pulled it out of his jacket and passed it around again. A waiter came by to collect their empty dinner plates as the music started again.

"I don't believe it," said Billy looking at the dance floor. "Ronald Anthony Wicker is dancing with Mary Brockton."

"What's his interest in Virgin Mary?" asked Anna.

"Maybe it's the challenge," said Billy. "The dance floor is so crowded I can't see them very well."

"What's going on?" asked Isadora. As they watched the tightly packed partiers on the dance floor Ronald Anthony Wicker doubled over and collapsed in spasms on the dance floor.

Chapter 2

A circle of curious dancers had gathered around the prone figure of Ronald Anthony Wicker. "Make way!" a man's voice. "I'm a doctor."

"That's Bushy Miller," said Anna. "He's barely a doctor."

"Bushy is just out of medical school," said Billy. "He's the closest thing to a doctor here I'm sure."

"Let's get a closer look," said Isadora as she and the two others made their way to where Bushy was kneeling down.

"Is he okay?" asked Isadora, Bushy looked up.

"I thought I recognized those sexy ankles," said Bushy with a grin.

"The cheek!" said Isadora pretending to be offended.

"To answer your question," said Bushy. "Ronald Anthony Wicker is dead."

"Are you sure?" asked Anna.

"I may be only just out of medical school, but I know dead when I see it."

The crowd parted as two men in white came

in carrying a stretcher. "No one is to leave here," said a rather good-looking man of about thirty. "I'm a police investigator and until we find out how this man died, no one is leaving here."

"That's Sergeant Starkey," said Billy.

"And how do you know him?" asked Isadora.

"It's a long story," said Billy who was blushing.

Isadora looked at the policeman. "You might want to take a look at that ice pick on the floor next to the body."

"What ice pick?" he asked.

"This one," she said as she pointed to an ice pick that had rolled under a nearby chair. "It could be the murder weapon."

"Murder!" someone in the crowd said and suddenly there was confusion as everyone began to speak.

"Keep your voice down," hissed Starkey. "We don't know if he was murdered."

"The blood on the floor," said Bushy as he turned the body over, "might be a clue."

"I'm going to take a statement from everyone," yelled Starkey. "I want to know who saw what." Starkey took out a handkerchief and picked up the ice pick.

Several uniformed policemen entered the ballroom and took statements from everyone. "I think I better go talk to Mary," said Isadora. "She seems very upset."

"Upset?" commented Anna. "She's balling her eyes out."

"Need I remind you that the man she was just dancing with died," said Billy.

"Her dancing wasn't bad enough to kill anyone," said Isadora as she headed over to Mary Brockton.

"It's been quite a shock for all of us," said Isadora as she put her arm around Mary's shoulder.

"Oh, but Izzy, they questioned me as if they thought I killed him."

"That's ridiculous. Why would they think that?"

"Because they said I was the closest to him and had the best opportunity to do something."

"They don't even know if it was murder," said Isadora who was convinced that it was indeed murder. "Come along, I'll take you home."

Anna was used to Isadora's driving, but Mary wasn't. She hung on for dear life as the car careened around corners and barely missed pedestrians. "Would you like us to come in and explain to your parents what happened?" offered Anna.

"Thank you," answered Mary, "but I better do it alone."

As Anna and Isadora drove off Anna turned to

Isadora, "What do you think is going on?"

"Well, we have two mysteries now."

"Two?" asked Anna confused.

"Yes, the murder of course, but I'm wondering what was going on with Billy and Sergeant Starkey."

"That did seem a little odd now that you say that."

It was after midnight when Isadora arrived home to find Rose waiting up for her. "How was the dance, Izzy?" asked Rose with a grin. "Some of those dances can be murder."

Isadora looked at her with suspicion. "I take it you've heard. I forget how fast the grapevine works."

"Betty Shaw called me as soon as she heard, and she heard it from Florence Greene, who heard it from…"

"Thanks Granny, I get the picture."

"That Wicker boy has always been trouble, still to be ice-picked at a dance is rather gruesome."

"He was dancing with Mary Brockton when he was stabbed. Mary is afraid the police think it was her."

"Mary Brockton? That's a laugh."

"She wasn't laughing."

"Poor girl, but what was she doing dancing with him?"

"He asked her. I don't think she gets asked

to dance too often," explained Isadora. "Well, I'm heading off to bed. Nothing I can do about anything now. Why are you all dressed up?"

"You're not the only one who has a social life."

"Well, I want to hear about," said Isadora yawning, "in the morning."

"Good night dear," said Rose who marveled at the fact that the young have such a detached concept of death.

Billy Brown and Sergeant Jeffery Starkey were sitting in a quiet corner of the Kennebec Diner having breakfast. "Aren't you afraid someone will see you?" asked Billy.

"I'm gathering information from a witness to a murder."

"What you gathered last night wasn't information."

"Keep your voice down."

"Back to the issue at hand," said Billy, "Izzy, Anna, and I were watching the dance floor, but it was so crowded that we didn't see who stabbed Ronald."

"I'd like the three of you to sit down and compare notes."

"You don't really think Mary Brockton could have killed him, do you?"

"She had the best opportunity, so she is a major suspect, but so is everyone at the dance."

"By the way," asked Billy looking carefully at

Jeff and hoping to get some reaction, "does your wife know where you were last night?"

"Yes," said Jeff with a laugh, "That is if I had a wife I would have said I was investigating."

"Yes, yes you were," he laughed.

Chapter 3

Isadora, with coffee cup still in her hand, hung up the telephone. "Who was that, Izzy?" asked Rose Garland as she watched her granddaughter's face change as she talked on the instrument.

"That was Billy. Sergeant Starkey wants to talk with the three of us."

"Starkey? Is he single?"

"I've no idea, why?"

"Well, you are around all these men, but I don't see anyone asking you to marry them."

"Granny, it's 1921 and women can even vote. Why would I want to get married?"

"I thought all of you girls wanted to find a husband."

"And who would I marry? Billy?"

"Izzy dear, I grew up in the theater and I can tell you Billy's not the marrying type."

"Yes, I did figure that one out. And as far as getting married, I don't believe you got married at twenty-one."

"Honey, I had men falling at my feet back then. Why would I want to get married? Every night the same dessert? Not me. Men are to be enjoyed, but not taken seriously."

"Sometimes Granny, you shock me."

"I doubt that very much. I've seen the blankets in the back seat of your car. Last time I checked you can't drive a car from the back seat, and it's summer and too hot for blankets."

"Sometimes it gets cold," said Isadora blushing.

At that Rose burst out laughing.

The little conversation came to a halt when the doorbell rang, much to Isadora's relief. Rose got up to answer the door and came back with Bushy Miller in tow. "There's a doctor here for you, Izzy. I didn't know you were sick."

"Very funny, Granny."

"Bushy would you like some coffee? I've made a fresh pot."

"Yes, thank you, Mrs. Garland. That would be wonderful."

"Here you go," said Rose pouring Bushy a cup of steaming brew. "Now if you two will excuse me, I need to freshen up. The ladies and I are going for lunch and then bridge."

When she left the room, Isadora turned to Bushy. "Why are you here?"

"I thought you might like to know what the medical examiner found out about Ronald Anthony Wicker."

"Medical examiner?"

"Old Doctor Joe. He's all we have around

here."

"That man is older than God. So what's the verdict?"

"Death by misadventure."

"I could have told you that," Isadora was enjoying sparring with Bushy.

"The thing is," continued Bushy, "that he had already been stabbed. And the wound shouldn't have been fatal."

"You better explain," said Isadora completely confused.

"Apparently he had been stabbed earlier, because during the autopsy it was discovered that the wound had been bandaged up."

"You mean he got stabbed and came to the dance? Then what killed him?"

"He was poisoned"

"How?"

"They are working on finding that out. Dr. Joe has called in an expert on poisoning."

"This is all very weird," she said as she set down her empty coffee mug.

"Well, it's up to the police to figure it out now."

"Speaking of the police, Sergeant Starkey wants to talk to Billy, Anna, and me."

"There's something wrong with that man," said Bushy.

"Who? Starkey?"

"Yes, Starkey. He comes from money and doesn't need to work, and he becomes a policeman? Tell me that's normal."

"Maybe he likes to work," said Isadora, but she didn't believe it.

Isadora, Anna, and Billy were sitting in the police "conference" room. "I want to know what the three of you saw," said Sergeant Starkey.

"Wicker came into the dance, spotted us and came over to talk to us," said Billy. Isadora noticed that Billy and Sergeant Starkey avoided looking at each other.

"What did you all talk about?" asked Starkey.

"Ronald only came over to annoy us," said Anna.

"No love lost there," added Isadora.

"But we didn't kill him," said Billy.

"No one said you did," stated Starkey. "Continue."

"Well, he then went over to talk to some Brunswick girls," said Isadora.

"Do you know who they were?"

"One of them was Betty Keys," said Anna. "We don't know who the others were."

"Yes," Starkey informed them. "Miss Keys is well known to the police, as are her friends. What did you observe about their conversation?"

"Now that you say that," said Isadora, "Betty looked angry, and the other two made faces. He left laughing and headed over to ask Mary Brockton to dance."

"Was there anything unusual about their dancing?" asked Starkey.

"There certainly was," huffed Isadora. "Ronald Anthony Wicker was a womanizer. Mary Brockton isn't the type that interests Ronald."

"It might surprise you to learn," Starkey informed them, "that he and Mary Brockton had recently become engaged."

There was silence in the room as the three friends took in the information. Finally Isadora broke the silence. "What?"

"You sound surprised," observed Starkey.

"He was engaged to Virgin Mary?" asked an incredulous Anna Greyson.

"Yes, his parents confirmed the fact," Starkey informed them.

"Well," speculated Billy, "they both come from money, and lots of money."

"That's all for now," announced Sergeant Starkey. "If I have any more questions I know where to find you."

Once they were outside the police station, they all broke into laughter. "Ronald Anthony Wicker and Mary, the virgin, Brockton," gasp Billy. "Oh, I can't stand it!"

"We shouldn't laugh," said Isadora as she laughed so hard, she couldn't catch her breath.

"By the way," Anna said as she turned to Billy, "what's going on with you and Sergeant Starkey?"

"Are you lovers?" asked Isadora.

"What an absurd question," said Billy as he walked off and left the two girls.

"Was the question absurd," asked Anna, "because they are, or is it absurd because they're not?"

"Notice he didn't deny it," said Isadora.

"No," agreed Anna, "he didn't."

Chapter 4

Rose Garland, dressed in a turban and embroidered robe looked like a gypsy fortuneteller, which in fact she had played on the stage more than once in her career. She was having "lunch" with the ladies, their "lunch" consisted of sandwiches and whiskey as the four of them played poker. Betty Shaw was winning, but Rose was holding her own. Florence Green, however, was losing. Rita Cornish, dealt out the next game.

Rose watched the others carefully. While Rose had a good poker face the others didn't. She looked at her own hand. It was time to go all out and raise the stakes. Betty Shaw and Florence Green were out. It was a show down between Rita Cornish and Rose.

"Full house," said Rita with a smirk.

"Four Queens," said Rose as she gathered the pot.

"So what do you know about the murder?" asked Florence. "Your granddaughter was there."

"Well, he was stabbed with an ice pick, but that was before the dance. At the dance he was poisoned, That's according to Izzy."

"Ice pick? Poison? Someone wanted him dead," said Betty.

"I'm sure there's a long list," added Rita as she poured more whiskey out to the players.

Mary Brockton sat in the parlor of her family's house on Washington Street. Isadora was taken to the parlor by a uniformed maid. She had never been inside the Brockton house before. Despite its location and outside appearance, Isadora took note of the shabby furnishings. Perhaps, she thought, the Brockton's were not as well off as they pretended to be.

"Thank God you are here, Izzy," said Mary who jumped out of her chair when Isadora entered.

"How are you doing?" asked Isadora who was surprised that Mary had called her.

"I'm okay, I guess."

"You don't sound very convinced."

"Oh, Izzy! I think Sergeant Starkey thinks I killed Ronald."

"I doubt that, but is it true you were engaged to Ronald?"

"I guess it is. But you see it was sort of arranged by both my parents and his."

"Sort of arranged. My God Mary, arranged marriages are archaic! Why would you want to get married to him?"

"I don't, I mean I didn't. It's that both families

are well off and both families are Catholic."

"I'd keep that bit of the story to yourself. Getting married off to someone you didn't like could be considered a motive for murder." A look of alarm crossed Mary's face. "You didn't tell that to Starkey did you?"

"I did. I thought it best to be honest. If they think I killed him, they'll hang me!" She burst into tears.

"Maine abolished the death penalty back in the 1880s, so you don't need to worry about that."

"Oh, Izzy! You have to help me." pleaded Mary. "My parents will pay you."

"Why me?" asked Isadora taken aback.

"Because people talk to you and they like you. You can find out things the police can't. No one is going to talk to the police willingly."

"Hmm, Isadora Drake, private detective," she said and then decided it sounded good. "I'll do it."

Isadora took out the only black dress she owned. The hem was a little too high for a funeral, she thought as she slipped it on, but it's the only black dress I have." She looked in the mirror and realized that black was a good color for her. "It's a little too plain," she said out loud. She reached into her top dresser drawer and pulled out a long string of pearls. Satisfied that the pearls made the dress stand out, she looked in her closet for a hat to go with the outfit. She saw a black wide-brimmed hat with a red flower on the side. She put it on and secured it with a hat pin and was pleased with the effect.

"Isadora Drake," yelled her grandmother Rose up the staircase, "are you ready to go?"

"Coming," she yelled back and descended the stairs. "What do you think?" she asked as she twirled around."

"I think you look a little too sexy for a funeral, and good for you."

"Don't you think that feather in your hair is a little too festive?" asked Isadora looking at her grandmother's black hat with the large white plume.

"Funerals are too grim," said Rose. "These Catholic funerals are longer and grimmer than a good protestant send off."

"I've never been to a catholic funeral," said Isadora thinking about her parents' funerals and how short the services had been.

"How's your Latin?" Rose asked.

"Pretty good, at least what I remember of it. Let's go and get a good seat. I want to see who shows up."

"Hmm, something is up with you," said Rose looking carefully at Isadora.

"I'm going to find out who killed Ronald Anthony Wicker. I've decided to become a detective."

Isadora and Rose had a good seat where they could observe the mourners. St. Mary's was filled with an ocean of black, and Isadora knew many of the faces. What connection some of them had with Ronald she couldn't figure out. She suspected that many of them had come just out of curiosity. She also suspected that not all of them were mourning the loss of Ronald Anthony Wicker.

"Nice legs," said Bushy Miller as he sat down in the pew next to Isadora.

"Nice knees, too," Isadora shot back and raised her skirt just about mid knee level. Bushy was taken by surprise and couldn't think of a comeback.

"Behave, you two," whispered Rose as the organ music started.

Anna Greyson, dressed in a more conservative black outfit, spotted them and sat down next to Bushy. "There's a lot of people here," she whispered. "You think he had this many friends?"

"Most likely they just want to make sure he's dead," Bushy whispered back.

"Behave," whispered Isadora as the coffin was wheeled to the front of the church.

Isadora, not the most spiritual of the attendees, rolled her eyes as the service in Latin continued. Seeing that, Rose gave her an elbow. Anna looked at Isadora and tried unsuccessfully to stifle her giggles. Bushy looked bored and started twiddling his thumbs which was too much for Anna and she fled the church before she burst out loud laughing. "That poor girl, said a woman sitting behind Isadora, "the funeral was too much for her.

She must have loved poor Ronald."

That was too much for Isadora and she had to take out a handkerchief and stuffed it in her mouth hoping those behind her would think she was wracked with sobs and not laughter. Much to her relief the service was winding up. She and her grandmother stayed seated so Isadora could see the mourners as they left the church.

/ Chapter 5

The four "bright young things" as young post-war adults were called, gathered at the New Meadows Inn for lunch after the funeral. "Your outfit is just a little too daring for a funeral, don't you think?" asked Billy.

"It's black," protested Isadora. "And besides Ronald Anthony Wicker may be dead, but I'm not. Just ask the doctor here."

"Isadora Drake," said Bushy Miller, "is most definitely alive."

"How come no one commented on my dress?" asked Anna Greyson.

"You look lovely," replied Billy, "in a very understated way."

"Thanks, I think." Anna didn't know if that being "understated" was a good thing or not.

"Since we are all together," said Isadora as she reached into her bag, "I have an announcement."

They all looked at her and Billy spoke up, "What now you crazy flapper?"

"I've decided to go into business," she replied and handed out business cards.

"Are you going to be a high-class courtesan?"

asked Billy.

"Read the stupid card!" answered an exasperated Isadora. The card read:

Isadora Drake
Private Inquiries
Phone: Hilltop 434

"Is this a joke?" asked Bushy.

"No, and I already have a case."

"Case? What case?" asked Billy.

"Mary Brockton has hired me to find out who really killed Ronald Anthony Wicker."

"A detective?" asked Anna clearly impressed.

"Would you like to be my sidekick?" asked Isadora, "You know like Dr. Watson is to Sherlock Holmes."

"This is silly," said Bushy Miller.

"I detect," replied Isadora, "a note of doubt in your voice. You'll see, and I detect a very delicious chicken dinner is heading my way," she said as she spied the waiter heading their way with a tray of food.

Bushy looked closely at Isadora. "I think she's serious."

"Of course I am. Who better?"

"Almost anyone," spouted Billy.

"So, what's the deal with medical school," asked Anna to change the subject.

"I'm done," answered Bushy.

"Done?" asked Isadora intrigued.

"I graduated at the top of my class."

"So, what will you do now?" asked Billy.

"I'm going to take over old Doc Joe's practice as he retires."

"So, you're going to be around?" asked Isadora with new interest.

"Oh, yes, I'll be around."

Bushy Miller got out of the shower, looked in the full-length mirror, and was satisfied with the image. He knew he was attractive, but was he attractive enough for Izzy Drake? So far, she's treated him as a friend and nothing more. He picked out his best suit, grabbed some breakfast, and headed off to church.

The Winter Street Church, an imposing white Gothic structure, loomed in front of him. Inside he spotted Izzy sitting with her grandmother. "May I sit with you ladies?" he asked Rose.

"Of course, Doctor Miller," answered Rose. She patted the area between herself and Izzy.

"You are looking lovely, Miss Drake," he whispered as he sat between the two ladies.

"You're not bad looking yourself, Doctor Miller."

Was she flirting with me, thought Bushy? "Good attendance today," he said not knowing what to say. Just then the organ prelude began.

After services Rose invited Bushy to Sunday dinner. Izzy began to look at Bushy in an all new light. Groomed and dressed, he no longer looked like the awkward teenager he had been before he went off to college.

"Are you still intent on being a detective?" Bushy asked her when they left church.

"Of course," she answered.

"Don't waste your breath," added Rose. "My granddaughter has a mind of her own."

"So, I've noticed," he said walking with them.

"Any more word about Ronald Anthony Wicker?" Izzy asked.

"He's still dead," answered Bushy.

"Very funny."

"Well, you're the one who is supposed to be investigating."

"It's a beautiful day," said Rose trying to change the subject.

Isadora shot her a look. "I sense Granny that you are up to something."

"Me, dear? Why ever would you think that?"

"Because she's a detective," said Bushy with a laugh.

Anna Greyson watched Isadora pull her Oldsmobile up to the sidewalk where she jumped into the car. As Isadora drove away Anna turned to her, "where are we going?"

"We are going to see Mary Brockton. She should be somewhat calmed down by now."

"Upper Washington Street makes me nervous. All those rich people and all the monstrous houses."

"Nonsense," said Isadora. "the more they have

the more trouble it brings. The Brockton's have nothing to be snotty about. After all their daughter is a prime suspect in the murder of her fiancé."

Before Anna could reply Isadora pulled up in front of the big white mansion. "I guess money can't buy good taste," said Anna as she looked up at the house.

The two walked up to the front door and rang the bell.

The door was opened by a uniformed maid. "May I help you?" the maid asked in accented English.

"Miss Drake and Miss Greyson here to see Miss Brockton.

"I'll see if she's home," said the maid as she scurried off.

"Why do they say it that way? asked Anna. "They could be honest and say 'I'll see if she wants to see you?'"

Both ladies were surprised to hear rapid footsteps just before Mary Brockton appeared. "Thank God you are here. Do you have any news?"

"It's a work in progress," answered Izzy.

"It's coming along," added Anna. The truth is that they had only discussed the case and speculated on who could be the murderer.

"We came to ask you a few questions," smiled Izzy, though she still believed Mary was involved somehow. "So, tell us about your relationship with Wicker."

"What do you mean?"

"I mean," said Isadora meaning business, "everything from the beginning!"

"My parents invited the Wickers over for dinner and Ronnie was with them."

"Ronnie?" asked Anna.

"He insisted on having me call him Ronnie."

"Continue," Isadora thought the story was coming to a climax.

"After dinner he asked if I should like to take a walk with him. I was flattered by the attention. He asked me for a date. He is, or rather was very handsome you know. I know what others think, but he was nice to me."

Izzy and Anna had a hard time conjuring up an image of Ronald Anthony Wicker as a nice guy.

"Then what happened?" asked Anna who was beginning to become interested."

"We dated for a few weeks; we even went to mass together."

Isadora rolled her eyes. "And then what?"

"Then he asked me to marry him. I was very happy at the time. Then I overheard my parents and the Wickers talking and then I realized this was an arrangement to marry the fortunes and that Ronnie had agreed to the plan."

"Then what did you do?"

"I ran down stairs and confronted them all. They made it clear that I was to marry no matter what, or I'd be turned out on the street."

"Good God, that sounds so Victorian," said Anna in shock.

"You realize," said Isadora, "that you have just given me a motive for murder."

Chapter 6

The bad weather had held off for weeks, but on Wednesday the sky opened up and a deluge of rain poured down on the town. Billy Brown, Anna Greyson, Isadora Drake sat in the corner of the speakeasy. Millers speakeasy. The speak was well known and since the leaders of the town were frequent guests, the chances of being raided were next to none.

"So how is the investigation going?" asked Billy.

"We interviewed Mary Brockton again yesterday," answered Izzy.

"What did you learn?"

"I can't tell you. I've been hired to prove Virgin Mary innocent."

"You think she's still a virgin?" asked Billy.

"I doubt it now," said Anna. "After all she dated Ronald Anthony Wicker. He's not one to whom a girl says no." Just then there was a commotion at the door.

"Oh. Look," said Billy. "It's the Bang sisters."

"Must they always dress alike?" asked Anna.

"Apparently so."

"But they don't even look alike," observed Izzy.

"Here they come," whispered Billy

"Well, lookie here," said Dora Bang "If it isn't the bitches."

"Now there are five," said Izzy.

"Please have a seat, Ladies" said Billy as he stood up as correct manners required. Izzy gave him a look. Debbie and Dora took a seat.

"I hear," said Debbie to Izzy, "That you're trying to become a detective."

"I'm not trying at all. I'm doing it."

"Interesting," added Dora. "What's your interest in the murder? Were you in love with Ronald Anthony Wicker."

"Hardly. I'm being paid."

"Paid?" laughed Debbie, "that's rich."

"Yes, I'm being paid. You all know about being paid, if you get my drift."

"Ooh," said Dora. "the lady has grown claws."

"You two were there that night," said Billy, "I saw you two on the dance floor on my way to the men's room."

"What of it?"

"You weren't there when the police questioned everyone."

"We left when we saw the commotion," added Debbie.

"How convenient," said Anna.

"What do you care?" asked Dora.

"Because you were on the dance floor, but of course if you'd rather tell the police…"

"Fine, we were dancing and when we saw Ronnie collapse, we left before the police showed up. We didn't want to get involved," explained Dora.

"Who were you two dancing with?" asked Billy.

"We didn't catch the names," replied Dora with a challenging look.

"I suspect," said Izzy with her own challenging look, "that both of you danced with Ronald Anthony Wicker."

"It might be wise of you," said Debbie, "to mind your own business."

When Isadora arrived home, she was surprised to find Bushy Miller having afternoon tea with Rose. "What ill wind blew you here?" she asked.

"Your Grandmother invited me for tea."

"How kind of her," said Izzy giving her grandmother a look. Rose just smiled.

"Please excuse me," said Rose, "But I have another engagement. "Offer our guest more tea." Rose made haste to grab her hat and get out of the house.

"Curious," commented Izzy.

"Lucky development," added Bushy. "I wanted to hear about your case."

Steady girl, she said to herself as she looked into those deep blue eyes. "I just finished interviewing the Bang sisters."

"Bang sisters? You better fill me in."

"Debbie and Dora are sisters who always dress the same even though they're not twins. Supposedly they are local entertainers and actresses but I have a feeling their form of entertaining is not socially approved. They've been in Bath a long time and nobody remembers their real name."

"Okay. But what's the real story. Why interview them?"

"They were at the dance the night Wicker was murdered."

"So? There were a lot of people, including us."

"They ran out just before the police arrived. Anna saw them dancing with Wicker once at another dance. According to Anna, they had a fling a while back."

"Both sisters? How interesting. Are you going to tell the police? They sound like suspects."

"I suppose I'll have to find Sergeant Starkey."

"I suppose you will. Do you need a ride?" offered Bushy.

"I can drive myself, and I need to pick up Anna. I'm not going alone."

Driving the Oldsmobile was a pleasant task for Isadora. It gave her a freedom that she had always wanted. She screeched to a halt in front of Anna's house. With some trepidation Anna climbed into the passenger seat and she had barely enough time to sit before Isadora hit the gas pedal and was off. Anna held on for dear life.

At the front desk of the police station Isadora asked for Sergeant Starkey. She and Anna were taken to a small office where Starkey was reading through police files.

"Well, well, if it isn't the flappers. What do you two want?"

"We have some information about the Wicker murder. Do you want it or not?"

"Don't get your pearls in a twist. Now tell me what you know." said Starkey. Isadora related all she had learned about the Bang sisters.

"The Bang sisters," said Starkey, "are not unknown to the police. Do you know where to find them?"

"Yes, they are usually at the...uh well.."

"The speakeasy? Please everyone knows about it, including the police."

"They do?" asked Anna.

"You think police don't like a drink now and then?" replied Starkey.

"I suppose," said Anna.

"Well, ladies, I need to go talk to the sisters. Thank you for coming in."

"Sure," said Isadora, "anytime."

Chapter 7

Billy Brown listened carefully as Isadora related the tale of the Bang sisters. "And how did Sergeant Starkey react?" he asked.

"Not the way I expected. He actually was interested in the conversation."

"Really? I find that hard to believe, but he is a good guy deep down."

"It must be buried way down deep," said Isadora. Billy had no follow up to that.

"Anyway," said Billy changing the subject, "the community theater is going to hold auditions for the new play they are doing.?

"So?"

"So I think we should audition for the play."

"Have you lost your marbles?"

"Come on, Izzy. It will be a blast."'

"Who else is auditioning?" asked Isadora.

"Me, Bushy, and Anna."

"Bushy?" asked Isadora with interest.

"He's trying for the lead."

"Come to think of it, it might be fun," she said with a faraway look on her face.

Sergeant Jeff Starkey was at the end of his abilities, he admitted to himself. "What are you thinking about?" asked Billy Brown. They were having breakfast at the Sagadahoc Diner.

"I'm getting nowhere with the Wicker murder."

"How come?"

"I have suspects, but no clues and certainly no evidence. And I definitely don't need your girlfriend Miss Drake interfering with the investigation."

"So, who do you have as suspects?"

"Well, Mary Brockton is number one," said Jeff. "After all she was dancing with him."

"You really think she's a murderer," asked Billy.

"Anyone can be a murderer. But I doubt it. Then thanks to your friend we now have the Bang sisters."

"That's not their real name," Billy liked to indulge in gossip. "That's their professional name."

"And what profession is that."

"Supposedly they are entertainers. They sing and dance at bars, but I suspect that isn't their main source of income."

"I'll have to have another talk with them," said Jeff.

"You're a cop. They aren't going to tell you anything."

Rose Garland looked at her granddaughter,

"You're going to do what?"

"I'm going to audition for the play."

"Good for you," Rose gave Izzy a smile. "Theater runs in the family."

"It's just community theater," Izzy reminded her.

"That's how I got my start in life; in more ways than one."

"Really Granny you are shocking. Most grandmothers bake cookies or sit in rocking chairs in their dotage."

"You think these legs are the legs of someone in their dotage?" Rose lifted her dress to illustrate her point.

"I guess not."

"Now," announced Rose. "I have a date tonight. Don't wait up."

Dr. Bushy Miller held the script in his hand and read the lines. Isadora and Anna looked on as Bushy projected his voice out into the theater. "He's very good," whispered Anna.

"Hard to believe that this is the same Bushy we grew up with," whispered Izzy. "Skinny and awkward."

"He's not awkward now," Anna said approvingly.

"Miss Greyson you're next," yelled the director Nathan Ward.

"Here goes nothing," Anna sighed.

"You'll be fine."

As Anna headed up the aisle, Billy Brown entered the theater and sat down next to Isadora, "How is she doing?"

"Not bad," whispered Izzy. "You just missed Bushy's reading. He was quite impressive."

"Good thing it's not a musical. That girl can't sing for toffee."

"It does have some musical number," Izzy informed him. "The play is filled with circus music."

"Were going to take a short break" said the director. "When we return Mr. Brown and Miss Drake will be up."

"Well isn't that the berries!" exclaimed Billy.

"How bad was I," asked Anna as she returned.

"You were wonderful," replied Izzy with only a slight exaggeration.

"Billy?"

"Sorry, Ducks, I only just arrived."

"Where did Bushy go?" asked Izzy.

"Maybe he went off to deliver a baby," Anna suggested.

"He went to the men's," Billy informed them.

Just then Bushy Miller rushed into the auditorium. "Have you heard the news," Bushy asked them.

"What news?" asked Izzy.

"Mary Brockton has been arrested for the murder of Ronald Anthony Wicker!"

Chapter 8

I sadora looked at Bushy Miller, "That's ridiculous! Who told you that?"

"I heard it from the source, Jeff Starkey."

"Jeff?" asked Billy not looking happy. "I didn't know you two were on a first name basis"

"I'm now Bath's doctor since Old Doc Joe retired. We have to work together since I am now the coroner as part of my job.

"Mr. Brown," said the director as he reentered the theater, "you're next."

"Wish me luck," whispered Billy as he got up the head to the stage.

They watched as Billy read his lines. His reading was good, but not great. To their surprise the director asked Billy to sing. Billy looked panicked for a moment, then stepped forward, listened to the music and began to sing. Billy's smooth tenor voice surprised everyone. Izzy, Anna, and Bushy began to clap.

"Miss Drake it's your turn," came the voice of the director.

"I'm dead if they ask me to sing," she whispered as she rose from her seat. She headed up the aisle to the stage as Billy headed back to his seat. "Nice job," she whispered as she passed him.

"Good luck," he whispered back.

Isadora seemed to float up the steps to the stage, took the script she was handed, stepped forward, and began reading.

"Great expression" said Bushy as he watched her. "Not to mention her delicate movements."

"Thank you everyone," said the director. "We'll post the names of the cast winners on Tuesday when we've completed tryouts."

"Let's go to the Speak," suggested Bushy. "I need a drink."

Sergeant Jeff Starkey took Isadora Drake to the lower level of the police station where the newly arrested Mary Brockton sat in a dreary cell. Isadora was shocked at the starkness of the jail.

Mary appeared almost catatonic until she saw her visitor. "Izzy," she practically yelled, "thank god you are here."

"I'm sure we can sort this out."

Starkey open the cell door to let Isadora in with Mary. "Give a shout when you're ready to leave." he said to her as he shut the door. For a moment Izzy panicked as the lock on the cell door clicked. She couldn't imagine how Mary felt.

"Mary, tell me what happened. The police won't tell me anything," she said as she sat down on the bunk next to Mary.

"The police said they have new evidence.

They came to the house and put me in handcuffs in front of my parents and then carted me out to the wagon for all to see."

"Your parents will no doubt get you a good lawyer. It's the weekend so the court won't be open until Monday, but I'm sure they'll have you out by then."

"Would you do me a favor, Izzy? Go over to St. Mary's and ask Father McKinney if he would come and see me?"

"Sure," she said as she rolled her eyes. "I'd be happy to," she lied. Mary didn't notice the light sarcasm.

St. Mary's was a yellow wood-framed building on High Street next to the high school. To Isadora it had an air of mystery. There were three steps up to the front door and Izzy managed to stumble and fall over all three.

"Are you okay?" asked a voice behind her as he managed to help her stand up.

"Fine," she lied as she turned around to see a man dressed in black with a white collar. As she tried to stand her ankle gave out.

"Come inside and sit for a while," the man said as he helped her inside the church, and sat her in a pew.

"Are you Father McKinney? she asked.

"The very same," he said. "What brings you to St. Mary's my child?"

"I'm here about Mary Brockton."

"A very devote young lady," he sighed. "I wish we had more, but it seems that since the war everyone is just out to have a good time. I'm sorry, you had something to tell me?"

"Mary is in jail," she told the priest."

"I'm sorry? You said she is in jail?"

"For murder."

It took the good father a moment to comprehend what Isadora had said. "I..." he was lost for words.

"She sent me here to ask you if you would be so kind as to visit her."

"I will go immediately," he said. "Are you able to stand?

"I think so," she said as she stood up and a searing pain went through her ankle.

"I'll drive you home on my way to the police station," he offered.

"Thank you."

Rose Garland watched as she saw a priest almost carry Isadora up the front walk. "What happened?"

"She fell on the church steps," he said as rose directed them to the front parlor. "I'm Father McKinney," he introduced himself.

"I'm Rose Garland, her grandmother." The two shook hands.

"I'm going to call the doctor," Rose said. "May I get you some tea?"

"Tea would be wonderful," he replied.

"Hey, I'm in pain here," complained Isadora.

"I've called Bushy," Rose informed her as she reentered the room.

"It's hopefully just a sprain," said the priest.

"You're awfully young to head a church, aren't you? You look like you are about my age," commented Isadora.

"I'm twenty-three," he replied somewhat annoyed.

"I'm twenty-one. My name is Isadora, in case you're interested. And do you have a first name?"

"Andrew."

"My question is," asked Rose. "What on earth were you doing at a Catholic church? No offense, Father."

"Non taken," he smiled.

"Mary Brockton asked me to find Father McKinney and ask him if he would visit her in jail."

"And I better take my leave and go see her."

"Thank you, Andrew, for helping me," said Isadora.

"You are welcome Isadora," he said as he headed for the door.

"What a waste," said Rose as soon as Andrew left.

"Why?"

"Are you blind? The man is gorgeous."

"So what?" commented Isadora. "He's a priest. He can't date or marry."

"Wake up Honey, he's just a man."

Much to Isadora's relief the doorbell rang.

The truth was that Isadora did notice how good looking the priest was. But Dr. Bushy Miller entered the parlor and Isadora couldn't decide which man was the better looking.

"I just saw a priest leave. Last rites might be just a little premature," he said feeling up her leg.

"That's not my ankle."

"Just checking out your reflexes," he grinned.

"Ow! That hurt," she said.

"The good news is it's only a sprain. You'll have to stay off your feet for a few days."

"A few days!" Isadora almost screamed, "There's a dance tomorrow night!"

"And you won't be dancing for at least a week or so. Doctor's orders."

"We'll see," said Isadora.

Chapter 9

Sergeant Jeff Starkey sighed as he watched Isadora Drake limp up the steps to the police station. He looked around for an escape route and found none. "What can I do for you, Miss Drake?" he asked with a sigh.

"For a starter you can let Mary Brockton out of jail. You can't really believe she murdered her fiancé."

"She has the best motive, being forced to marry someone against her will."

"You mean she has the best motive, so far."

"Any way, Miss Drake" continued Jeff Starkey, "she's out of jail thanks to her rich parents."

"My friends call me Izzy, and we both have Billy Brown for a friend."

"Call me Jeff," he said after he flinched at Billy's name. "As far as Wicker's death if you find anything else let me know."

"You want my help?" she blurted out in surprise.

"You may be able to find out more because you are not with the police."

"Okay. I should get going. I'm using up your

time." she said. "Have a good day, err Jeff.

"You, too, Izzy."

"What was all that about?" she asked herself aloud as she got in her car?

It was difficult for Isadora to drive with a sprained ankle but she got in her car and tried to ignore her pain. She remembered that the list of those who won parts in the play would be posted this afternoon.

"Isadora May Drake!" Rose Garland yelled at her granddaughter as Izzy walked through the front door. "What do you think you're doing out there driving with a bad ankle? It's not going to heal if you keep abusing it."

"I'm fine," she said though the truth was that her ankle was throbbing.

"Billy Brown called and asked you to call back. He's over at Anna's."

Izzy went to the wooden wall phone adjusted the mouthpiece, cranked the magneto, got the operator. "Is that you Izzy?" asked the operator. It was Bertha Clark, one of her friends. They chatted for a moment before she connected Izzy to the Greyson's house phone.

Billy and Anna were waiting on the front porch when Isadora drove up to the house where the two of them jumped into the front seat. "I'm nervous," said Anna. "What if you guys get a part in the play and I don't?"

"I suspect," said Billy, "that you'll live."

"I'm not even sure I want to be in the play," Isadora informed them. "The play is rather stupid, don't you think?"

"I rather like it," protested Anna. "I've always wanted to join the circus."

"Izzy is right," added Billy. "Boy meets circus girl, boy loses girl, boy gets girl back and they live happily ever after. It's been done."

"And here we are," said Isadora as she drove up to the theater.

Inside there was a small crowd gathered around the bulletin board. They had to wait before the three of them could get near enough to read the cast list. To Isadora's surprise she got the female lead. Anna got a role of a circus performer, and Billy got the part of the lead man's best friend.

"Bushy got the lead!" said Billy.

"That's the good news," Isadora pointed out a name on the list. "The Bang sisters got the entertainment parts. That's the bad news."

The four 'bright young things' were sitting in a booth having lunch at the Kennebec Diner. The play rehearsals at the Uptown Theater would start tomorrow night, and they were nervous. "Thank god I don't have many lines to learn," sighed Anna.

"I have the most lines," said Billy. "Even more than the hero."

"Let's change the subject," suggested Bushy.

"I agree," put in Isadora.

"Oh, I have something for you, Izzy" said Billy as he passed her a folded piece of paper.

"What's this?" she asked as she took the paper and unfolded it.

"It's a list of everyone at the dance."

"How did you get this?" asked Isadora. "Wait, you had to have gotten this from Sergeant Starkey."

"Jeff wanted to give it to you with the understanding that if you find something, you'll give it to him."

"Jeff?" asked Anna. "I didn't think you were that close."

"Jeff is our age," Billy said rather than address his relationship. "And to be a sergeant so young he has to be good at his job."

"Smooth," commented Isadora. Billy ignored the remark.

"And," continued Billy, "you don't know where the list came from."

"Got it," said Isadora.

"Izzy?" Bushy asked. "I have to hire a receptionist for my office. I was wondering if you'd like to work in a doctor's office?"

"I wouldn't have to do anything medical would I?"

"No, I'll have to find a nurse for that."

A look of concentration crossed her face. After all she really didn't have to work. But she was becoming bored with doing nothing, and Bushy was so good looking. "I'll do it," she said.

"Really?" Bushy couldn't believe his luck.

"Why do they call you Bushy?"

Billy had a mouth full of coffee, which he nearly choked on. "Oh, Izzy," he said gasping for breath because he was laughing so hard, "You are such an innocent."

"I'll tell you some day," promised Bushy with a wicked grin.

Isadora Drake sat in the easy chair by the window looking out at the garden. Since her grandmother had hired a gardener, the back yard was a riot of color. As she read through the list of suspects for the murder, or rather those who were there when Ronald Anthony Wicker keeled over on the dance floor. Surprisingly she knew most of the names on the list. She had to admit that she had no idea where to start. Maybe this detective thing was a bad idea.

"Why are you inside on this beautiful day?" asked her grandmother who has just walked into the room.

"Where have you been?" asked Isadora. "You were gone over night." Isadora had a very good idea where Rose had been.

"A lady never tells," she responded.

"No one said anything about a lady. You were either playing poker all night, or you met a man, or possibly both."

"That's a very limited choice." said Rose who reached over and pressed a wall button. "Would you like some tea?"

"That sounds great," said Isadora. Mrs. Baker, Roses housekeeper, came in with a pot of tea and a plate of finger sandwiches and quietly slipped away.

"I have news," said Izzy.

"I'm listening. Did you find the murderer?" asked Rose.

"Not even close. Bushy Miller asked me to be his receptionist."

"Did he now," laughed Rose. "Was it your inability to type or was it your medical background that attracted him?"

"I can sort of type," protested Izzy.

"Honey, he hired you because he wanted a pretty face at the front desk, and he wants to be near you for obvious reasons."

"What reasons?"

"Are you blind? He's in love with you."

"Don't be silly," she paused. "You really think so?"

"I do. Now how are you going to work for Bushy and still be a detective and be in a play?"

"I hadn't thought of that," Izzy admitted. "I'll think of something."

"You always do," said her Grandmother grinning. Rose enjoyed a little human drama for entertainment, especially if happens to someone else.

Chapter 10

Isadora stumbled out of bed remembering that this was the first day of working for Dr. Bushy Miller. She wasn't used to waking up so early. As she headed downstairs for coffee, she thought of all the stuff she will have to do. She would first have to remember to call him Dr. Miller in the office.

"Well, I've never seen you up this early," said Rose who already had a coffee cup in her hand.

"I don't like this," she replied. "I don't think I'm cut out for being a working girl."

"You might want to rephrase that."

"I knew as soon as I said it."

"So," asked Rose, "what's your day like?"

"I'll head over to the doctor's office and then after work I'm going to talk to a friend of Ronald Anthony Whicker."

"Why?"

"To see if I can get any information the police couldn't get. People don't like to talk to the police."

"No one likes to talk to the police," agreed Rose.

Bushy Miller's office wasn't new. He had bought the house where Old Doc Joe had his office in one wing of the house. Isadora had been given the key by Bushy so she could arrive and set up before Bushy was ready for his patients.

The office looked like a hurricane had laid waste to the outer office. Good morning," said a cheery Bushy Miller as he entered the office from outside."

"What," asked Isadora making a sweeping motion with her arm, "is all this?"

"Old Doc Joe left in a hurry. He sold me the house for practically nothing, packed up what he wanted, and left town all in one day. This is what he left behind."

"*Merde*," she said in French.

"I know some French, too," laughed Bushy, "such language!"

"Where do we start?"

"Anything that looks like a patient's record, place on the desk. And I need to remind you that anything you learn here is not to leave this office."

"I understand," agreed Isadora.

"All the other stuff in here is to be thrown out. Let me give you a tour of the place," offered Bushy.

"The house was built by Captain Josiah Greenlaw in 1850 in what was then the outskirts of town. Its architecture is Second Empire which you can tell because of the mansard roof. At some point the place was remodeled late Victorian. The two styles actually meld well together. In 1900 Doc Joe bought it and added a medical wing on the house."

"Handy," commented Isadora, "work where you live."

"Now if we proceed through that thick door, we'll be in the living area."

Bushy took her through the downstairs with its double parlor, library, dining room, and kitchen. The house was furnished with comfortable furnishings, but Isadora thought that it could use a woman's touch.

"Want to see the upstairs?"

"Why Doctor Miller, what are you suggesting?" she teased.

"I'm suggesting that there are three bedrooms, an elegant bathroom, plus an upstairs parlor."

"You are going to need a housekeeper with all this space," said Isadora.

"Do you know anyone?"

"I'll add that duty to my receptionist work," she told him. And silently she said to herself that the only housekeeper he is going to have will be some old crone. Who needs competition?

Isadora had managed to organize half of the files, much to Bushy's surprise. As she left his office she looked up at the clock on the Baptist church and saw that she had some time left of the day. It was time to pick up the investigation. She drove to Anna's house and picked her up.

"How was your first day of work?" Anna inquired.

"I spent it in the office separating patients records from trash. And I did a good job if I say so myself."

"So where are we going?" Wondered Anna who has a good idea of what was going to happen.

"I'm taking the list of names that Billy passed to me, and I'm going to question them."

"I was afraid you would drop this detective thing once you had a real job."

"This is a real job," Isadora defended herself.

"So, who are we going to see first?" asked Anna.

"Wicker's best friend Michael Frazer."

"Oh, he's a dreamboat," gushed Anna.

"A dreamboat who has the intellect of a stump."

"True."

They rode along with Anna hanging on for dear life as the automobile careened around the corner. Isadora pulled up in front of the First National Bank where Michael Frazer worked. After a brief inquiry with the head teller the two would-be detectives were directed to a small office.

"Izzy and Anna, this is a surprise," said Frazer as he rose from his desk and indicated two seats in front of his desk. "What can I do for you?"

Isadora passed Michael her business card, "I'm

looking into Ronald Anthony's death."

Michael Frazer looked at the card. "Is this a joke?"

"I assure you this is no joke. I've been hired by Mary Brockton's parents."

"I don't have any idea why he was killed or who might have done it," protested Michael.

"Nor do I," said Izzy. "I want to know about Wicker that night."

"Why me?"

"You came into the dance with him," added Anna.

"I drove him to the dance. He was too drunk to drive."

"What about his stab wounds?" asked Izzy. "Do you know who tried to kill him?"

"No one stabbed him," said Michael as he gave the two women a once over.

"What?" said a shocked Anna.

"The last time I checked," said Isadora, "Stabbing is often fatal,"

"Ron was drunk and he took out the ice pick to break up some ice for drinks. He hit the ice at the wrong angle and the ice pick bounced off the ice and he stabbed himself."

"And then what?" asked Anna.

"Then we took him to Old Doc Joe. He was packing up his office to leave town, but he bandaged Ron's wounds."

"Did you tell Sergeant Starkey about this?" asked Isadora.

"Why would I? It had nothing to do with his murder."

"And how would anyone know that. It made it look like two attempts to kill him."

"Well, if the stupid cop had asked me, I would have told him."

"Why did he have the ice pick with him?" asked Isadora.

"He wanted to tell everyone that he fought off an attacker and got the weapon away from the attacker and would show the wounds to back up his story."

"He's a piece of work," muttered Isadora. "Thanks for the information," Isadora said as she got up to leave."

"Oh, by the way Anna," said Michael, "are you busy tonight?"

"I'm not," she said smiling at Michael Frazer.

Back in the car the two rode in silence until Isadora broke the silence. "You're going out on a date with Michael Frazer? He's a bit dim."

"But he is gorgeous, and did you see that bulge?"

"Anna! You shock me."

"I highly doubt that!"

Chapter 11

Isadora picked up the ear piece of the telephone, cranked it two times and asked the operator to connect her with the police station. A brief conversation with Jeff Starkey, and he agreed to meet her at the Sagadahoc Diner.

She spied Jeff in a corner booth, walked over and took a seat. "I have some news," she said.

"So, you said over the phone. You could have told me then."

"It's a party line and people like a little entertainment by listening in," she told him.

"Good point. I thought you might bring Billy along for protection."

"I think Billy's the one who needs protection," she watched him carefully for a reaction. There was none.

"I interviewed Michael Frazer." She went on and described her meeting.

"He could be lying about the stabbing," said Jeff when she had finished.

"I don't think he's bright enough to come up with a story like that. Besides why would Wicker have the ice pick unless it was to impress girls who would believe him when he said he wrestled it away from his attacker?"

"What can I get you?" asked the waitress as she passed by their booth.

"Just coffee for me," said Isadora.

"Me, too," echoed Jeff. As she went to grab their coffee cups, he thought he heard her grumble "Big spenders." He laughed but turned serious. "I need to ask you something."

"What is it?" she was curious.

"I know you are no fool," he answered. "It's about Billy and me."

"Yes, I've figured it out." she looked at him not as a policeman, but as a man. Handsome face, almost too pretty for a man. Broad shoulders and piercing green eyes.

"Well, I need someone to take to dances and out to dinner."

"You want me to pretend to be your date?"

"I guess that's what I'm asking."

"So, people will think you're..."

"Yes." he said quickly." She looked startled, thought Jeff.

"Do we get to make out?" she asked with a grin.

"Probably," he answered and matched her grin.

"I'll do it," she said without hesitation. "But maybe limit it to occasional coffee and lunch dates."

"That," he agreed, "would be great."

It was hot and sticky weather and Isadora was glad that the new fashions let her arms be bare, and her legs bare to her knees. The rehearsal hall was stuffy and hot and there was a buzz of excitement.

"If I could have everyone's attention," shouted the director, whose name was Butch Whiley. A name, thought Isadora, that didn't belong to a fifty-something fat, bald man. "I want to introduce you to our choreographer, Miss Bancroft. There are several dance numbers in the show, and she's going to teach you the Charleston."

"What's the Charleston?" Anna whispered to Isadora.

"It's a dance that came out of the South," she answered. "It's very animated."

"Thank you, Mr. Wiley. Now if everyone would line up," said Miss Bancroft.

"She's at least sixty," whispered Billy to Isadora and Anna.

Miss Bancroft began to dance the Charleston and moved so effortlessly that everyone was shocked into silence. "Never mind," whispered Billy clearly impressed with the dance.

Isadora Drake looked at the clock and rolled out of bed. After cleaning up she went to her closet for an outfit for work. She wanted something that looked professional and yet something that Bushy Miller might notice. She picked out a pink and gray dress and wondered, not for the first time, why women's fashions dictated a flat chest look. She held the bust flattener in her hand, dropped it on the floor and kicked it across the floor. "Not today," she said out loud.

Rose had the coffee steaming in the stove as Isadora presented herself. "Something is different," commented her grandmother as she looked Izzy up and down.

"I've decided the flat look is not for me."

"Good for you honey. I never understood modern fashion. Let me get you some coffee."

"Yes, please. How does one make coffee?" asked Isadora with an embarrassed look.

"What do you mean how does one make coffee? You don't know how to make coffee? I fear your domestic skills are sadly lacking."

"I want to impress Bushy by having coffee ready."

"I see," replied Rose suppressing her urge to laugh. "Come here and I'll show you."

Dr. Bushy Miller was both nervous and excited as this was the first day of office hours. He was pleased at Isadora's work cleaning up the office and setting out supplies in the examination rooms. It wasn't lost on him that Isadora's figure seemed fuller than before, and she had coffee ready!

Having been given the job of finding a nurse, Isadora would be interviewing three candidates. The first was due to come in any minute. She didn't know how to interview a potential work colleague. Ask about nursing school and experience, she guessed. The first visitor was a man so she figured that he was a patient.

"Good morning," she greeted the gentleman. "Are you here for an appointment?" He certainly didn't look sick, she thought.

"I'm hoping to speak with the doctor," he said as he handed her a bunch of pens that said 'Reliable Medical Corp.' on them.

"He's with a patient right now," she lied. "I'll go check and see if he's available."

She entered Bushy's office. "There's a salesman here to see you."

"It didn't take any time at all for them to find me." Isadora handed him the salesman's business card. "Tell him I'm too busy to..." He stopped halfway through his sentence as he read the card. He sat straight up in his chair. "Tell him I'll see him."

Curious now she went back to the reception area. "The doctor will see you now."

"I knew he would," he said mysteriously as Isadora pointed out his office door.

She had several applicants for the nursing positions. She picked up the phone and made several phone calls to set up appointments. At ten o'clock the first applicant came in. Looking over her application Isadora ask her questions that Bushy had supplied. There was no doubt that the applicant was more than qualified for the job. "Thank you, Miss Brewster, we'll be in touch."

The problem was that Miss Brewster was a knock-out. Well dressed, great figure, killer smile, and blonde hair. "Who needs the competition," she said aloud.

"What competition?" asked Bushy as he came out to the reception area with the salesman following behind.

"Just talking to myself," claimed Isadora turning red with embarrassment.

"Izzy, this is Bob Miller, my cousin. We grew up together."

"Pleased to meet you, Mr. Miller,"

"Please call me Bob."

"Only if you call me, Izzy, like all my friends." She couldn't decide which cousin was the better looking. Bushy had close cut curly hair which he left natural. Bob had long straight hair that he slicked down with hair tonic for the wet look. Bushy, she decided, was the winner.

Chapter 12

Bushy had offered to drive Isadora home, but she had her Buick parked outside the office. She saw that it was afternoon tea time, but decided to forgo the afternoon ritual and work on the Wicker case. She had hoped the stabbing explained that Mary Brockton would be off the suspect list, but according to Sergeant Starkey, Mary has the best motive and opportunity. She dreaded the next interview, which was with Ronald Anthony Wicker's parents.

Isadora had never been inside the huge white mansion on Washington Street, but it was hard to miss. It was, in her opinion, the symbol of conspicuous consumption and an architect's folly.

She rang the front door and a uniformed maid answered the door. "Trades people to the back door," said the maid in a haughty manner. This was too much for Isadora.

"Listen, Honey," said Isadora grabbing the maid by the arm, "I don't enter anywhere but the front door. You go tell the Wickers that Isadora Drake would like to talk to them. Do I make myself clear?" Isadora push the maid well away from her.

The maid ran off saying, "Yes Miss."

Isadora smiled. She liked to set people straight who set themselves up as better than others. The maid returned and took Isadora into the back parlor of the house. She observed the furnishings that, unlike the Brockton's worn furnishings, seem new and expensive.

"Good afternoon, Miss Drake," said Fredrick Wicker.

"Oh, Izzy," said his wife Bertha, "it's just too much to take in."

Isadora, seeing the tears well up in her eyes, went over to the sofa, sat down and put her arms around her. "We all miss Ronny," she lied.

"I heard," said Mr. Wicker, "that you're looking for Ronny's killer?"

"You will find him, won't you?" blurted out Mrs. Wicker. "The police don't seem to be doing anything."

"I'll try my best," Isadora assured her. "If I may ask you both some questions." The two Wickers nodded. "Do you know anyone who would want to harm him?"

The two of them shot each other a look. "We don't want to accuse anyone," began Mrs. Wicker, "but Ronnie was having girl trouble."

"You mean because Mary was not in love with him?"

"No," added Mr. Wicker quickly, "he had a girl from Brunswick chasing him. Letters, phone calls and she even showed up here once."

"Who was she?" asked Isadora.

"We don't know," answered Mr. Wicker. "He wouldn't say."

"Were either of you home when she came here?"

"I was," said Bertha. "A very nasty piece of baggage."

"What did she look like?"

"I only saw her briefly but she was about five-five and rather well fed but not fat. She had dyed blonde hair. She was dressed rather shabby, and the way she spoke she was not of our class, if you know what I mean."

Isadora knew exactly what she meant. "Yes, I see," she said and she wanted to slap the class-conscious bitch. "Did you tell this to the police?"

"Good god no! They don't need to know our personal business."

"Mrs. Wicker," began Isadora, "your son was murdered. Any information, no matter how insignificant you might think it was, could be a clue." Isadora decided she didn't like these people. That was no surprise since she didn't like their son. "Anything else you think might be important?"

They both shook their heads.

"Thank you for seeing me," she said as she headed out the door and drove home.

The general commotion in the theater was normal, Isadora guessed, until rehearsal began. Bruce Whiley called the cast together and the commotion stopped. "I hope everyone studied their lines. Miller and Drake," he called out. "You'll be working with Miss Bancroft learning the Charleston. Those in the chorus line will work with me. The rest of you I want you to practice your lines with each other."

Bushy Miller felt like a awkward teenager as he tried to follow Miss Bancroft's directions. Isadora, on the other hand, had a natural grace about her and made the dance look effortless. "Dr. Miller," said Miss Bancroft, "you'll catch on. It's a very fun dance.".

"I hope so," he sighed.

Everything stopped for a moment when Billy Brown's voice soared into the air. Everyone who knew Billy had no idea of the beautiful voice he had. They listened transfixed as he sang the solo from the play. At the end of the song the theater broke out in spontaneous applause.

Billy looked embarrassed as he headed off the stage. Isadora spotted a movement on the balcony. It was Sergeant Jeff Starkey watching Billy sing. She knew she needed to see him about her interview with the Wickers, but she thought it might not be the best time to do that. Then she noticed Billy sneaking up the stairway to the balcony.

By the end of rehearsal Bushy Miller had improved greatly. He credited not Miss Bancroft, but his beautiful dancing partner. The Bright Young Things all headed out to the Hotel Dining room for a late-night supper after rehearsal.

Isadora and Bushy were the first to arrive and reserved a table. Anna was next and had the dim-witted Michael Frazer as her date. It appeared that Wicker's best friend already had a few drinks down at the speakeasy. Last to arrive was Billy Brown with, surprisingly, Sergeant Starkey.

"How did rehearsal go?" asked Jeff Starkey.

"You saw for yourself, Jeff," said Isadora. "I saw you up in the balcony."

"Billy's singing was the height of rehearsal," added Anna.

Billy had the humility to look embarrassed. "It was just a good song. Anyone could sing it."

The young waiter brought them the menus and brought them all a cup of coffee. Isadora watched the waiter walk away and noticed that both Jeff and Billy were watching the waiter, too.

"I'm not sure what the play is about," stated Jeff. "Rehearsal seemed to be all over the place."

"That's because we were rehearsing different scenes in small groups," Billy said.

"Oh, no," said Bushy as he looked across the room. "It's the Bang sisters."

"And they have two men with them," observed Anna.

"Two older men with them," added Michael Frazer, who until now had been silent.

"I wonder what they had to do for the men to buy them dinner," asked Isadora innocently.

"Take a wild guess," answered Anna and she

made a hand gesture which left no doubt about what she meant.

"Anna!" gasped Isadora trying to suppress a laugh. "That's shocking."

"She's right," confirmed Michael.

"How do you know?" asked Jeff.

"Ronnie often paid them for...er, entertainment."

The young waiter appeared and took their orders. This time everyone at the table watched the waiter walk away. "Interesting walk," said Bushy.

"He looks familiar," said Michael with a puzzled look.

"Does he now?" asked Anna looking carefully at Michael.

"Yes, now I have it," announced Michael. "I've seen him with Ronnie."

Chapter 13

Isadora was surprised when her grandmother Rose walked into the doctor's office. "Good morning, Granny. What are you doing here?"

"I have an appointment."

Isadora looked at her appointment book, and sure enough Rose was scheduled in. "Don't remember giving you an appointment?"

"Some detective. If you notice it's not in your handwriting."

Rose was right, she had to admit; it wasn't her hand writing. "But who...?" she asked. And before she could finish, the living quarter's door opened and out walked a pretty petite young woman with blonde hair.

"Good morning everyone," said the young lady, who looked about seventeen.

Isadora's head was spinning. Early morning, young lady, coming in from Bushy's apartment. Does Bushy pay for sex with teenagers? The rat!!"

"I'm Flora," she introduced herself. Something about Flora seemed familiar.

"Which one of you is Mrs. Garland?" asked Flora. "I made the appointment when you called after hours last night."

Isadora went into a murderous rage. Who did this little tart think she was? Did she look like someone's grandmother? The door to the office opened and Bushy flew in ready for the day. Isadora realized she hadn't made coffee. He'd get his coffee alright. Over his head or in his face! "I see you've met my sister," he said as he took Rose into the exam room.

Isadora felt foolish and relieved at the same time. "Little Flora? The last time I saw you, you were six years old."

"I've been away at boarding school for most of the time. I've finished school and I wanted to see my brother. Either he was away at medical school, or I was at school in Switzerland. I wanted to get to know him, so when he invited me here, I came as fast as I could."

"What are you doing for lunch?" asked Isadora trying to make up for her suspicious mind.

"No plans," she answered.

"We must do lunch then. I'm Isadora by the way."

"Yes, I know. My brother has told me all about you. You've made quite a conquest."

"I have?" asked Isadora, pleased to have that confirmation.

"Yes, and now I see why. You are the bees' knees."

"Well, I should get your brother his coffee."

"You know how to make coffee?" asked Flora.

"May I watch, Miss Drake?"

"I've just learned how to do it. And I thought I was the only one who never learned to make coffee," laughed Isadora. "And call me Izzy."

Flora carefully watched Izzy make coffee as if she were watching a magical act. Izzy poured coffee for the two of them as the door to the examination room opened and Rose and Dr. Miller came out together. "Healthy as a horse," said Rose. Bushy nodded in agreement.

"I see you two have gotten along," observed Bushy.

"Yes," acknowledged Flora. "In fact, we are having lunch together so we can talk about you."

"Watch out for Izzy," said Rose as she headed for the exit. "She's a wicked gossip."

"And from whom did I learn that, Granny?"

Isadora and Flora balanced themselves on stools at Baily's Lunch Stop. Noon time was always busy as the food was good and also cheap. "so, tell me about yourself," asked Flora.

"Not much to tell. I went to the Mitchell School and then on to Morse High. Both my parents died in the Spanish Flu epidemic. Just my older brother and I were left and Grandma Rose took us both in. My brother is an engineer at the Edison's Menlo Park in New Jersey. How about you?"

"I went to Mitchell, but then my parents sent me off to boarding school in England. I finished school two months ago. My parents relocated to New York City and both my brother and I hate the city.

"Your brother was ahead of me in school," Izzy told her. "Growing up he was rather awkward. It's hard to believe he's turned into such a handsome specimen."

"I know. I hadn't seen him in several years while I was away. We wrote to each other all the time while I was in England. Speak of the devil," said Flora as Bushy entered the lunch room.

"Talking about me?" he asked as he stood behind them.

"Don't flatter yourself." quipped Izzy.

Bushy took the stool next to Isadora. "Maybe you can show Flora around town," he suggested.

"That will take all of ten minutes," Isadora shot back. "What about going on a date that's not a date?" she asked Flora. "Get to see the sights without some man trying to get fresh with you?"

Bushy and Flora looked at her like she had gone bonkers. "Are you having a stroke?" asked Bushy. "I should go get my black bag."

"Here's what I was thinking," she said and went ahead and explained her plan.

Isadora was exhausted by the time she arrived home. The housekeeper was getting dinner ready, and as Isadora went upstairs to change, she saw Rose sitting at her dressing table expertly putting on makeup. It was clear that her many years on stage had taught her all about illusion.

"You look ten years younger," Isadora told her.

"Just ten? I was hoping for twenty."

"You must have a date."

"Honey, I may be a grandmother, but I'm not dead yet. Men are fun. You should get you one."

"What would I do with a man?" asked Isadora.

Caught by surprise, Rose almost choked. "If you don't know what to do with a man yet, you should ask your friend Anna. That girl gets around." Which reminded Isadora of the time when Anna said virginity was overrated.

"She does?" Anna never talked about dating.

Rose shook her head and then changed the subject. "Are you going off detecting tonight?" she asked.

"No. I'm staying home. I'm too tired to do much. I'll listen to the Victrola and then go to bed."

After settling down, Izzy curled up in a big easy chair with a book and watched her grandmother leave. Is her grandmother really a floozy or is she just colorful?

Isadora woke ready to face the day and, in her mind, she went over her wardrobe planning what she would wear. It was going to be a hot day and then she realized it was Saturday and she didn't have to go into work. Bushy only handled emergencies on the weekend and she was free.

She grabbed her Japanese kimono and slippers and headed to the bathroom, combed her hair and went downstairs where Rose was sipping tea.

"Good morning dear; how did you sleep?"

"I slept very well, thank you. I didn't hear you come in." The housekeeper passed Isadora a steaming cup of coffee.

"It was a late night," said Rose with a smile. "The morning mail came, by the way."

"Anything interesting?" asked Izzy.

"A letter from your brother."

"Peter? How is he doing?"

"He's coming home."

"I guess it's that time of year for his vacation."

"No, he's coming home to stay." Caught by surprise Isadora almost spit out her coffee.

Chapter 14

Mrs. Baker, the housekeeper, packed up a picnic lunch for Isadora and her friends. Izzy drove to pick up Anna and Billy. Bushy said he needed to stay around in case of emergency, but his sister Flora was delighted to go with them. Much to Isadora's relief, Sergeant Starkey was scheduled to be on duty.

Isadora drove down to the ferry terminal and waited in a long line of cars. "They are planning to build a bridge sometime," said Billy

"Can't be soon enough," sputtered Isadora. They could see the ferry *Governor King* heading back from the Woolwich side of the Kennebec river. Luckily, they were the last car to drive onto the ferry.

As soon as they got off the ferry, Isadora drove toward Georgetown to an area with pink sand beaches. When they reached a nice shady spot close to the ocean, Isadora parked the car and Billy unloaded the sling chairs and made a circle under an ancient pine tree.

The fresh air, the smell of the ocean, and the magnificent view, seemed to have increased appetites. Mrs. Baker, who knew all about young people, had packed a lunch of fresh cucumbers, fried chicken, macaroni salad, biscuits, fruit salad, and a fresh strawberry pie.

"That was a picnic," said Billy as he relaxed in his seat.

"What we need now is some music," said Anna. "Billy, go get the Victrola out of the car."

"That's what I get for being the only male in the group," he sighed. He went to the car and picked up the small record player and a box of records. Isadora picked out a record, and Billy put the record on the turntable, wound up the machine, and placed the arm on the record. It was a classical piece and the group relaxed as they finished the coffee Mrs. Baker had packed in thermos bottles.

"So, Sherlock and Watson," said Billy when the record had ended, "How is the investigation going?"

"Investigation?" asked Flora, who knew nothing of the murder of Ronald Anthony Wicker.

Anna quickly explained what she and Izzy were up to. "And that's about it."

"You two are real detectives?" she asked impressed.

"I guess we are," admitted Isadora.

"My money is on the Bang sisters," said Billy.

"Or a jealous girlfriend," said Isadora.

"I just thought of what Michael Frazer said at dinner the other night," remembered Anna whose face lit up at the thought. "He talked about the waiter."

"Waiter?" asked Billy.

"Yes," continued Anna. "He said he had seen Wicker with the waiter."

"And you think the waiter did it?" asked Isadora.

"I didn't say that," protested Anna. "I just think it's interesting."

"Enough of this," declared Isadora. "Billy put this record on the turntable," she instructed him. "Now Anna and I are going to teach you all to dance the Charleston."

Sunday morning proved to be one of those June days when the sun shone brightly, the flowers were in bloom, the air was filled with floral scents. Rose and Anna walked to church where the whiteness of the Winter Street Church seemed to glow like alabaster in the sun.

As they walked along, they were joined by Bushy and his sister Flora. "Good morning ladies," He greeted them. "Mrs. Garland, this is my sister Flora. Isadora you already know."

"Pleased to meet you Mrs. Garland. Izzy has told me all about you."

"Have you indeed, Izzy?" said Rose feigning irritation. "Don't believe everything she says."

"It was only good things," Flora tried defending Izzy.

"In that case it's all true," everyone laughed.

Ahead of them were couples and families

walking up the steps of the church and mingling with each other and the single older parishioners. The church bell rang and everyone began to fill the pews. As Izzy and the others entered the church the organ prelude began. The hymn numbers were displayed on two boards on each side of the church so everyone would know what they would be singing. Izzy recognized two of the numbers and sighed. The hymns were more patriotic as the fourth of July approached, and Izzy, not for the first time, wondered what was happening at the Central Congregational Church down the street.

At the end of the service many members stayed behind to chat with other members, but Izzy suggested getting out into the fresh air and no one objected at all. Rose invited Bushy and Flora to join them for Sunday dinner.

When they arrived back home Izzy noticed a Ford Model T parked on the street, and the front door open. "Looks like we have a guest," observed Rose.

"And I have a good idea who it is," added Isadora.

"Peter! This is a surprise," exclaimed Rose when she spotted him in an easy chair with the Sunday paper.

"Granny!" he greeted her as he bounced out of the chair. "And Izzy!" he gave them both a hug. Bushy and Peter shook hands. They had been in the same class and were friends growing up.

"You probably don't remember my little sister Flora."

"Flora? But you were just a baby the last time I saw you."

"Surprise," she replied.

"I'll go tell Mrs. Baker we have three guests for dinner," said Rose as she headed off to the kitchen.

Dinner was truly a feast and Mrs. Baker had outdone herself. As the meal and the conversations continued, Rose had a chance to observe her dinner guests. It was clear that Peter was interested in Flora and that Izzy was interested in Bushy. She knew Bushy was very interested in Izzy from her conversations with him, but the two of them acted like brother and sister, and that wasn't going anywhere. What was wrong with young people? She just shook her head.

"You've been very quiet, Granny," observed Peter.

"You know what they say; better to seem a fool than to open your mouth and prove it."

"You are many things, Granny," said Isadora, "but you are no fool."

"So, Peter," asked Bushy, "When are you going back?"

"I'm not," said Peter to everyone's surprise.

"What do you mean you're not?" asked Isadora. "You work for Thomas Edison!"

"That's just it," he replied. "It's *work for...* and Edison isn't who you think he is."

"So what will you do?" asked Rose looking concerned.

"I'm going to open a radio store."

"Here in Bath?" asked Flora who until then had little to say.

"Radio is just a fad," added Bushy.

"Radio," replied Peter, "is going to be the next big thing. You wait and see."

"Who wants dessert?" asked Mrs. Baker as she brought in a cool looking strawberry meringue pie.

The morning was already hot when Isadora opened up the office. It was damp and stuffy and she opened the window, turned on the newly bought fans, which Isadora thought too expensive, and went to make coffee and found that the coffee had already been made. Flora apparently had been up early.

The phone began ringing and Isadora set up the appointments for the day. "How's the nurse search going?" asked Bushy as he walked into the office with a fresh cup of coffee.

"I'll get on it right away," said Isadora who had forgotten to set up more interviews.

Isadora had set up appointments for the day and sat back to enjoy her coffee. She reached into the files and pulled up the resumes for the nurse's position. The one that stuck out the most was from an Ivy Bloom. Reading the name, she rolled her eyes, but as she scanned the page she saw an impressive list of experiences, and even better was the fact that she was forty, and not a threat to her.

For a moment her mind wandered. Bushy was clearly interested in Izzy, or was he? He hadn't made any advancement; he hadn't even kissed her for goodness' sake.

She picked up the phone and dialed Mrs. Bloom and they agreed on a time for an interview. She had only a little bookkeeping to do, and decided to review the Wicker case. She wrote down the main events. Wicker had accidentally stabbed himself, old Doc Joe had stitched him up, and Wicker decided to use his wounds to impress people that he had defeated his attacker. He had gone to the dance at New Meadows with Michael Frazer, and it was clear that Wicker had had a few drinks already.

She and Anna had sat down to eat and Billy Brown joined them. Wicker spotted them and came over to harass them. Then he went to a table where the Brunswick girls were sitting. Apparently, they weren't all that happy to see him either. To everyone's surprise he asked Mary Brockton to dance. As they danced, he suddenly collapsed on the dance floor and died.

Bushy Miller was there to declare him dead. She stopped for a moment. Bushy was at the dance? She wondered who his date was. Then later she had learned that the Bang sisters had been at the dance and left before the police came. She had also learned that Wicker had been a "friend" of the Bang sisters. And the waiter that Michael said he had seen with Wicker. Suddenly she remembered why he looked familiar. He was working at the New Meadows Inn at the buffet that night.

"Ready for lunch?" said Bushy interrupting her thoughts.

"Where are we going?"

"My place," he answered. "Flora has made lunch."

Chapter 15

s they went through the office door connecting the office with the living quarters, the smells were delightful and they could here Flora working in the kitchen. Isadora was surprised to find her brother Peter in the parlor.

"What are you doing here?" she asked him.

"I was invited."

Flora poked her head into the room. "I thought four would be a more balanced number than three," she said looking almost embarrassed. Peter smiled at her and she was blushing. "And luncheon is ready.

Flora had made a cold potato soup, chicken aspic, pickled beets, and cold ham. Perfect for a hot summer day. With it she served switchel, also known as haymaker's punch.

Isadora had never had switchel, and one taste of it made her make a face. "A bit tart isn't it," she asked.

"It is a drink that farmers take with them when they are working in the fields," Bushy explained. "It's full of potassium. And it does quench a thirst. It's made of vinegar, honey, and ginger."

"Actually," Izzy said after her second taste, "it's not that bad."

"This soup," said Peter in an effort to change the subject, "is wonderful."

"When did you ever learn to cook?" asked her brother Bushy. "I never saw you near a kitchen when we were growing up."

"We had to learn to cook at boarding school," she explained. "And how to run a household."

"No algebra or chemistry?" asked Izzy, a product of Morse High School.

"We did learn French and painting. They were educating us to be good wives."

"Sounds kind of limiting." Isadora made a face.

"So, Peter," broke in Bushy to change the subject, "how's the business going?"

"I've rented a store on Front Street. The one that used to be a shoe shop. That business moved down a block."

"When do you open?" asked Flora batting her eyes.

"I've ordered the goods. They'll be here by rail in a week."

"We don't even have one at home," Izzy reminded her brother.

"Ours will be the first one I'll install."

"I understand," said Peter looking at Izzy, "that my sister styles herself as a detective. What do you all think of that?"

"She's actually worked with the police detective on the case," Bushy defended her.

"I think she's wonderful," added Flora. Peter had no reason to contradict Flora, so he let the subject drop.

"Who do you think did it?" asked Flora who was not ready to let the subject drop.

"My money is on the Bang sisters," said Isadora.

"Why is that?" asked Bushy.

"Because I don't like them," she said seriously and then laughed.

"Flora, lunch was wonderful," said Bushy, "but Izzy and I have to get back to work."

"Yes, Flora, thanks for lunch," added Izzy.

"I'll help you with the dishes," offered Peter, and was awarded with a smile from Flora.

It was Isadora's job to filter out the applicants for the nurse's position. Mrs. Welby was a kind, if rather large woman. Izzy went over Mrs. Welby's work experience. "And why are you interested in this job?" Isadora asked. "You have glowing recommendations from several hospitals. You could work anywhere."

"I grew up in Bath and I have two sons I want to raise here. And I'm tired of hospital work. I can do more good working with one patient at a time rather than twenty on a hospital ward."

Isadora open the door to Bushy's office. "There is a Mrs. Welby who is interested in the nurse's job. I think you need to see her."

"Send her in. What do you think?"

"It's up to you, but I think she's the one." She went back to the waiting room. "Dr. Miller would like to see you."

"Wish me luck," she said as she went into Bushy's office.

Left alone Isadora had time to think. The dress rehearsal for the play was tomorrow night. They had had only six rehearsals and Isadora wished they had another six to go. It also bothered her that she had made little progress in clearing Mary Brockton of the Wicker murder. What to do next?

She picked up the phone and called Betty Keys, one of the Brunswick girls who had been at the dance. She had had words with Ronald Wicker and Izzy was interested in what that conversation was. Much to her surprise Betty agreed to meet her at a coffee shop in Brunswick.

In a very short time Mrs. Welby came out of the doctor's office. Isadora looked up and saw a very grim looking woman. "How did it go?" she asked.

"Well," she said seriously, "he asked a lot of questions."

"And?"

"And," she paused a moment and then broke out in a smile, "I got the job!"

"Congratulations, Mrs. Welby," as Isadora got up to shake her hand.

"Please call me Judy. After all we will be working together."

"Only if you call me Izzy. When do you start?"

"Tomorrow. Now I have to find a nurse's outfit. I'll have to go into Portland shopping."

Isadora drove into Brunswick found the Starlight Tea Room. Betty Keys was already sitting at a table and waved Isadora over. They both ordered tea and a plate of tea pastries. "I'm surprised you wanted to talk to me," said Isadora.

"Something has been bothering me and I'd rather tell you than the police."

"I'm listening."

"You were at the dance so you saw Ronnie when he came over to our table."

"Yes, I did. He didn't have a very warm reception if I interpreted correctly." Just then the waitress brought their tea and pastries.

"I'm afraid he didn't, but you know how arrogant he was. There was a girl at our table that I didn't know very well. She was a friend of one of my friends. Her name was Kathy something. I didn't get the last name. She had a bad reaction when Ronnie came over; she started calling him names. It was clear that they knew each other if you get my drift."

"Oh, yes, I got it."

"Well, when Ronnie first came into the dance, this Kathy person saw him and muttered something like 'he's going to die.' I didn't think much of it at the time. And then Ronnie died on the dance floor and all hell broke loose. The shock was too much for most of us, and it was only the next day that I remembered her comment. I mean we all say things we don't mean, but there was something in her voice. But I can't go to the police. They already think of me as a trouble maker. They'll think I'm making it up. I thought if I told you, you could go to the police.

"But then I'd have to tell them that I got the information from you. Can you talk to your friend and get her last name?"

"If she even knows it, but I'll ask."

"Great, then let me know." Isadora had no idea what she would do with the information if she got it, but she'd think of that later.

Chapter 16

The atmosphere could only be described as frantic as the cast prepared for dress rehearsal. Isadora sat in one of the makeup chairs in front of a huge, long mirror. Anna, Bushy, and Billy were seated next to her as the makeup artists worked on them. The other cast members were already made up. Izzy thought they all looked comical with dark pancake and rouge. Bushy was objecting to putting on lipstick, but in the end the makeup person persuaded him to wear it.

Once they got into costume they quietly sat and waited for the show to start.

"Places everyone," yelled the director.

Isabella could hear the cacophony of musicians tuning up. Everyone who was in the opening act took their places on the stage. Billy Brown would lead a parade of clowns around the stage as circus music played in the background.

The overture finished and the curtain went up. Billy was dressed as a lion tamer and circled the stage followed by the clowns. After three circles on the stage the clowns filed out and left Billy alone on stage. Billy stepped forward and sang the first song of the play. "The whole world is a circus," he sang and then walked off stage.

Bushy Miller, dressed as the ring master was in the back of the theater and ran down the middle aisle shouting for the crowd to come to the big tent for the greatest show on earth.

The show continued and was an eclectic mix of different scenes in the life of the circus. It was the first time that each scene was played in sequence. Isabella and Bushy had only seen the scenes they were in. Watching the other scenes when they weren't on stage they had to admit they liked the musical, while not great theater, was at least entertaining.

At the end of the play the director commented on the performance. Billy needed to project more. Anna had to move faster when her cue came, the Bang sisters needed to work on their timing. Bushy and Izzy needed to speed up the Charleston number, and the lighting crew needed more lights at the opening scene.

"Rest up," the director told the cast. "We open the day after tomorrow."

After the rehearsal the gang went for a late supper at the River Hotel by the waterfront. There were three couples, Isadora and Bushy, Anna Gray and Michael Frazer, Jeff Starkey and Billy Brown. "I'm exhausted," Isadora complained."

"Well we both worked all day and then had a

long rehearsal," agreed Bushy.

"I can't wait to see it. I bet Anna is great in it," added Michael.

"She is," agreed Bushy."

The conversation was interrupted as the Bang sisters entered the dining room and walked by the table. "You all did a great job," said Dora much to the surprise of everyone.

"Your dance number was great, too," said Billy who was rewarded with a smile. The waiter took them over to a table across the dining room.

"What was that all about?" asked Anna.

"That was nice of them," said Billy. "I didn't catch any sarcasm."

"That must have cost them some pride," remarked Isadora.

"They're up to something," added Anna. "I don't trust them."

"Nor should you," said Jeff. "Those two ladies, and I use the word loosely because we are in polite society, are shady characters.

"Finally," said Izzy, "the food is here. I'm starving."

The night was dark with no moon as Bushy drove Anna and Izzy home. Anna was dropped off first and Bushy waited until she was safely in the house. "I'm done in," said Izzy as she yawned.

"Get some sleep," said Bushy. "We have a busy day tomorrow. I have patients all day, and Mrs. Welby will be starting."

"Will having a nurse make things easier," she asked as Bushy eased the automobile back on the street.

"When I examine women, I need a nurse in there with me to make things proper. That's why I've asked you several times to come into the examination room with me."

"I thought it was because you wanted my company."

Bushy pulled over to the side of the road and stopped the car. Izzy wasn't sure why he had stopped the car until he grabbed her and slowly kissed her. Izzy had read in novels about going weak in the knees when a woman was kissed. She had doubted it was real and thought it was just a fanciful fiction by romance writers, but she was discovering that it was a real thing.

"I couldn't wait any longer," whispered Bushy.

"What took you so long?"

"I wasn't sure how you felt about me."

"You are the ideal man. You are so good looking and smart. You have a great sense of humor, I've never seen you angry or upset," she replied.

"And I'm a doctor," he added.

"I'd have fallen for you if you had been a ditch digger." This time she kissed him.

"I better get you home before I lose all control."

In her mind Izzy was picturing what it would be like if he did lose control. It wasn't an unpleasant fantasy.

Rose Garland watched as Isadora stumbled to the dining room for breakfast. She gave Izzy the once over and smiled.

"What are you smiling about?" asked Izzy who was trying to wake up.

"I think someone was with a man last night. You have that look."

"Bushy finally kissed me," admitted Isadora.

"Well, it's about time. I despaired of you both going around like brother and sister."

"I wanted to do more than kiss him," Izzy admitted.

"And that's a good thing."

Chapter 17

Izzy, in her half-sleep remembered what it was like to have kissed Bushy Miller. She smiled sat up in bed, and stretched her arms out. Everything had changed and then the thought occurred to her that she worked for Bushy. Would that be awkward?

She headed to the bathroom to clean up and then went to the closet and picked out the outfit for the day. She sighed as she looked at her clothes. There are so few colors that look good on a red head she thought to herself. Finally, she settled on a white dress with black trimming. It was a bold style and she hoped Bushy would like it.

Her grandmother and brother were already at the table having toast and coffee. Mrs. Baker brought in the breakfast plates and they all tucked into their meal. "I like the dress," Peter said to her when they had finished breakfast and were on their second cup of coffee.

"I hope Bushy likes it," Izzy said.

"The only part of the dress," said Rose, "that he's going to be looking at are your titties."

"Grandma!" This was one of the few times

that Izzy had been truly shocked. Peter, when he heard his grandmother had had a mouth full of coffee and he spewed it all over himself. He was laughing so hard that Izzy punched him in the arm.

When the room had quieted down Izzy spoke to her brother. "What are you doing today?"

"I've got inventory arriving today and I can start fixing up the store."

"You think you can sell enough radios to make a living?" she asked.

"You'll be surprised. Everyone thinks it's just a fad," he replied. "But you wait; it's going to be the next big thing."

Isadora was the first one to open the office. She was nervous. How would Bushy act at the office after last night's kiss? The door opened and in walked Mrs. Welby. She was dressed in all white and looked every inch the quintessential nurse that she was.

"Good morning, Izzy," she said with a bright smile. "I can't wait to start."

"Good morning Judy," replied Izzy. "Bushy, er... Dr. Miller usually comes in at eight-thirty."

"I'll make some coffee," offered Mrs. Welby.

"I hope you are better at it than I am," admitted Izzy. She pointed to the little store room where the coffee pot was kept.

She brought in two cups and passed one to Isadora and they sat in two of the waiting room chairs. "Dr. Miller is very handsome," commented Judy Welby. "He's going to get a plethora of women for various 'illnesses'."

Isadora was about to reply when Bushy walked into the office. "Good morning Miss Drake and Mrs. Welby."

"Good morning Doctor," replied Izzy. So that was how he wanted to play it, she thought. She could see the laughter in his eyes.

"Are you ready for tonight, Miss Drake?" he asked Izzy.

"Tonight?" she was confused.

"The play is tonight," he reminded her.

"You're going to a play?" asked Mrs. Welby. "How exciting!"

"We're not going to it," informed Izzy. "We are in it."

"Oh, wonderful. I'll have to drag my husband to see it. I can't wait to see it."

"Now," said Bushy, to Mrs. Welby. "We have our first patient coming in at nine, so let me show you around."

The back stage of the theater could only be described as chaotic panic. Isadora couldn't imagine that out of all the chaos that a smooth performance was possible. The small orchestra was warming up adding instrumental pandemonium to the confusion. "Places everyone," the director shouted and the men and the women filed out of their dressing rooms. In makeup and costumes they looked almost like a professional cast.

Billy brown's face was white with terror as he would be the first one to appear on stage. The house lights went down, and the stage lights went up. Billy heard the music start up. He thought he was going to be sick. The curtain opened and much to his surprise he forgot all about the audience and began to sing, as the circus performers gathered on stage and joined him.

"This is getting too real," whispered Isadora to Bushy as they waited for their time on stage.

"We'll be fine," Bushy whispered back.

As Billy and the circus performers filed off stage, Bushy and Isadora walked on stage and spoke their first lines. By the third act Isadora felt more comfortable and even was enjoying herself more than she believed possible. At curtain call she practically glowed with the applause of the audience.

Once the audience had filed out of the theater, the sets were removed and a huge cake was brought out along with a washtub full of ice and what appeared to be buried in the ice was bootleg wine and beer. Everyone went silent when Sergeant Starkey appeared backstage. He walked up to the ice bucket. Looked it over as if looking for evidence, pull out a beer, grabbed an opener, and took a swallow. Everyone relaxed and conversations continued.

He continued on over to where Bushy, Isadora, Billy and Anna were standing. "Great job everyone," he said but he was only looking at Billy.

"Funny trick," Bushy told Jeff Starkey, "You had everyone panicked thinking this was a raid."

"When was the last time anyone place in this town was raided?" asked Jeff.

"The police raided the speakeasy last month," said Anna who had been present at the raid.

"And what did the police find?"

"They didn't find anything," said Anna. "Someone had warned the place earlier. It gave us all time to put everything away."

"I wonder," said Jeff with a wicked grin, "who warned them?"

"I'm going to guess it was you," added Bushy.

"The police are expected to raid any bootleg or speakeasies they can find," explained Jeff. "The fact that they didn't find anything doesn't negate the fact that to the public's eyes they were doing their job. After all police like their booze, too."

"And since we are all here," added Izzy, "and the play is over let's celebrate!"

The party was going in full force and the heat of the night combined with the heat of human bodies made for a sweltering atmosphere as the cast party continued. "My it's stuffy in here," Isabella whispered to Anna.

"Let's go out and get some air," suggested Anna.

"Great idea," Izzy replied.

Though warm outside, the air had a slight breeze and seemed fresh compared to the crowded backstage of the theater. The two sat down on the front steps of the theater when they spied someone walking toward them.

"I've been looking for you," said Betty Keys.

"Good evening, Betty," said Anna in a less than friendly voice. "You bored of Brunswick?"

"I came to see Izzy," Betty replied ignoring the jibe.

"Anna," Izzy said, "Betty is helping with the case. She had some valuable information."

"And I have more."

"Do sit down," suggested Izzy, "so I don't have to get a sore neck from looking up to you." Betty took the suggestion and sat down on the steps with the other two.

"I really enjoyed the play. You were both very good. I really wanted to join the circus when I was a kid, just to get out of here."

"Sometimes I feel the same way," said Anna trying now to be nice.

"Anyway," continued Betty, "I have the last name of that Kathy person from the dance at New Meadows."

"The one who threatened to kill him?" Izzy had almost forgotten that bit of information.

"Her name," she claims, "is Kathy Smith."

"Smith?" asked Anna, "Sounds fake to me."

"Anyway," Betty went on, "I have a plan."

"I'm listening." Izzy hoped it would be a good

plan.

"My friend and I are going to invite Kathy for luncheon. You could happen by and we'll invite you to join us. Then we'll have the opportunity to question her about her relationship with Ronnie. She's the type that will jump at the chance to talk about it."

"Betty, that's a brilliant idea," said Izzy.

"You think so? Thanks."

"Why are you doing this?" asked Anna suspiciously.

"Everyone thinks I have a bad reputation. I'm looking to redeem myself."

"And if we find the real killer, you'll get part of the credit," promised Izzy.

"There you are," said Bushy as he loomed around the corner. "Ready to go home?"

"I sure am," smiled Isadora. "I need my beauty sleep."

Isadora Drake and Anna Greyson sat in the police station waiting to talk to Sergeant Starkey who was in a meeting with the police chief. When he appeared Isadora could tell something was wrong?

"Something bothering you?" asked Izzy.

"I'm getting pressure to solve the Wicker case," he said. "He thinks we should proceed with the idea that Mary Brockton is the killer."

"That's ridiculous," Izzy said making a face. "She's no killer."

"I agree," replied Jeff Starkey, "but the chief is getting pressure from the Wicker family, and they are rich and powerful in town."

"You mean he'll arrest an innocent girl just to end a case?" Anna was incredulous.

"His reasoning is that if she is innocent," explained Jeff, "that the jury would find her not guilty."

"Even if she wasn't found guilty, she would be ruined. People will think she got off because her parents are rich." Izzy was outraged.

"So why are you two here?" Jeff asked mostly to change the subject.

"I have a theory," claimed Isadora.

"Of course, you do." Jeff rolled his eyes.

"I saw that."

"Okay, go ahead." He sounded skeptical.

"When I interviewed Betty Keys..."

Jeff held up his hand to stop her. "Betty Keys is hardly a reliable witness."

"Are you going to listen or are you going to keep interrupting me?"

"Okay, go ahead."

"Let me start at the beginning. Ronald Anthony Wicker was at the dance at the New Meadows Inn. As he was dancing with Mary Brockton he collapsed on the floor. It was initially believed he died of stab wounds. According to his best friend Michael Frazer those wounds were self-inflicted when Wicker was showing off. The medical examiner, who in this case was old Doc

Joe, the wounds were not serious enough to cause death."

"So far everything you've told me I already know," interrupted Sergeant Starkey.

"I'm getting to the good parts," she told him.

"Fine."

"When he first came into the dance, and this is the important part, he went over to the Brunswick girls' table. There seemed to be some type of commotion. So, when I talked with Betty Keys it seems that at the table was a young woman who was not a regular member of Betty's group. Her name was Kathy Smith."

Isadora saw a glimmer of recognition in Jeff's eyes. "Yes," he confirmed, "I've heard the name."

"Any way," continued Izzy, "According to Betty and one other witness this Kathy Smith seemed to recognize Wicker. This Kathy person started yelling at Wicker. After he left, she said something like 'he's going to die.'"

"She was the one," said Anna thinking back to the dance, "who dropped Wicker's flask." Jeff and Izzy looked at her with shock. It was so quiet Anna had no idea what she said.

"What did you say?" asked Sergeant Starkey.

"Wicker had a flask he passed around," Anna remembered, "when it was passed to her, she fumbled and dropped it."

"Did she drink from it?" asked Jeff.

"I don't think so," said Anna thinking back. "I think she passed it back to him."

"Do you know what this means?" asked Jeff.

"It means," said Izzy, "what she had was the opportunity to slip poison into the flask."

"But what was her motive?" Jeff knew there had to be one.

"I think I can help you out with that," said Izzy. "According to Michael Frazer, Ronnie was being stalked by one of the girls he dated. When I talked to the Wickers, they told me that some crazed girl showed up at their house. If we can prove it was her then you'll have motive and opportunity."

"If you bring her in for questioning," suggested Anna, who had been mostly silent, "you could get a photograph of her and show it to the Wickers."

"And just who," Jeff was a little miffed to be told what to do by a civilian, "is the police detective here?"

Chapter 18

Mary Brockton was surprised to see Isadora and Anna approaching the house. She hoped it was a good omen, but the way her life had gone recently she braced herself for bad news. "Come in," she said as they came to the door. "let's go to the parlor."

They entered the parlor and each chose a chair. As soon as they settled Isadora began her news. "You'll be happy to know that you are off the suspect list."

"Are you sure?" Mary couldn't believe her good luck.

"Yes, a more likely suspect has been identified," added Anna.

"Where are my manners?" said Mary as she reached over and pushed a bell to summon the maid. When the maid appeared, Mary requested tea for her guests.

"Your parents will be pleased," said Anna.

Mary turned to Izzy, "I'm so relieved. Thank you both so much. I'll make sure Dad writes a check before you go. What will you do now the case is closed?"

"The case won't be closed until Wicker's murderer is arrested. I plan to make sure the killer is caught. The Wickers, however distasteful they are, deserve to have justice."

The tea arrived and Mary poured out the tea and offered her guests the fresh baked cookies the maid had brought up. "Excuse me a moment," said Mary as she ran down the hallway.

"What was that about?" asked Anna.

"I think she went off to tell her parents the good news."

When Izzy and Anna were on their third cookie Mary returned with an envelope. "Here is your payment," Mary handed the envelope to Izzy.

"Thank you." Izzy wanted to tear it open, but she knew it would be rude to open it now. After a brief conversation Anna and Izzy excused themselves. Once in the car Izzy held up the envelope. "My first payment as a detective.!"

"Open it," demanded Anna.

Izzy tore it open and looked at the check. She was shocked to see the amount. Silently she passed the check to Anna. "Wow!" Anna was shocked. "That's a lot of money."

"Enough for both of us," replied Izzy who planned to drive to the bank that very minute.

Returning home Izzy was surprised to see a big wooden box on a table in the parlor. There were four dials in front and a big horn on the top. Her brother Peter was fiddling in the back.

"What's that?" she asked.

Peter poked his head around to look at her. "It's a radio."

"I know what a radio looks like," she said.

"It's an Atwater Kent," he explained to her. "It's their most powerful model. It has four tubes." Izzy wasn't sure what the significance was but she didn't ask. "I just strung a long wire aerial in the back yard," he continued. "With any luck we'll have music and news in an hour or two."

Sergeant Jeff Starkey rolled his eyes. "So what is this plan of yours?" he asked Isadora in a way that left no doubt that he was being sarcastic.

"We girls, that is Betty Keys and I are going to invite this Katy Smith to lunch."

"That's nice," he rolled his eyes again.

"Let me finish and if you roll those eyes again, I'll have to slap you. During lunch the conversation will move into talk about what a horrible person Wicker was. Hopefully this Kathy person, who I think is off balance will, most likely incriminate herself somehow. And you'll be behind a screen listening to the whole thing."

Jeff turned to her with his full attention. "It's a long shot but it might work."

"Great, I'll get things moving," said Isadora. Anything you want to share with me?"

"Fine. When I showed the Wickers the photo of Smith, they confirmed that Kathy Smith was the one who showed up at their house."

"But that's just circumstantial evidence isn't it?" she asked.

"Yes, that is why we need more."

"Well, I should be going," said Izzy as she got out of the chair. "By the way I haven't seen Billy for a few days. Tell him I said he needs to come around more. I'm sure you'll be seeing him soon. Probably tonight I'm sure."

Sergeant Jeff Starkey was speechless and red in the face.

"Bushy called you," said Rose when Isadora returned home. "And since it's Saturday I'm sure it wasn't about work."

"Did he leave a message?"

"Yes, he said come to dinner. His sister will be cooking and your brother was also invited. Just think, if things progress with both you and your brother, Peter might end up as your brother-in-law."

"You're being a bit premature don't you think?"

"Nonsense. I know what happens when young people get together."

"I bet you do," countered Izzy.

Isadora looked into her closet and sighed. If she was going to move forward in her pursuit of the handsome doctor, she would have to dress up to impress. At the back of her closet she found just the dress. It was a black dress with black beads that shimmered. The black fringe along the bottom of the dress was made up almost exclusively with black beads. She found a black headband to go along with the outfit and added a white plume. She finished off the outfit with a long string of white pearls.

As she headed downstairs, she ran into her brother Peter. "Why are you all tarted up?" he asked.

"The same reason you're wearing a new suit and slicked back your hair." Unlike herself, Peter had light brown hair that was curly and that even hair tonic couldn't tame. "Flora will be impressed."

"That's what I'm hoping. No doubt the good doctor will appreciate your appearance tonight."

"I hope so. Want a ride? My car is newer."

"Sure. Nothing impressive about my Ford."

"Look at you two," said Rose as she came down from upstairs.

"Got a date, Granny?" Peter asked. Rose was dressed in her colorful long dress and matching turban.

"Yes, and don't bother waiting up for me, if you get my meaning."

"Loud and clear, Granny," Peter laughed.

Rose headed out the door and the two siblings ran to the window. A very large black automobile pulled up and a man hopped out of the driver's seat and opened the door for Rose.

"Who is he?" Peter asked his sister.

"I've never seen him before."

"You think you're a detective; you should find out."

"For your information I am a detective, and I'll investigate."

"Or," said Peter, "you could just ask her."

Chapter 19

Isadora hoped that her plan would work as she sat at a table in the New Meadows Inn. At her back was a large Japanese folding screen. "Where are they?" whispered Jeff Starkey from behind the screen. "It's hot back here."

"It's hot everywhere. Now be quiet they're here."

Betty Keys came into the dining room looking very fashionable in a new suit and hat. By contrast Katy Smith was dressed like a tart. Her hemline a little too high and her neckline a little too low, and for God's sake she had so much makeup in that she could have passed for a clown.

"Glad you all could make it," said Isadora as the two guests sat down.

"Thank you, Izzy. It's good to see you." Kathy just grunted.

The waiter came over to take their order. They started off ordering a coke, and when the three glasses were delivered Isadora drew out a flask from her handbag. She poured a generous amount into Kathy's glass, and pretended to do the same into Betty's glass as well as her own.

"Any luck on the Wicker case?" asked Betty to steer the conversation in the right direction.

"There are so many who seem to have hated him," Isabella informed them, "that it's almost impossible to narrow it down."

"He was rather a nasty piece of work," added Betty.

"He got what he deserved," added Kathy who took a large gulp of her drink.

"He certainly was one for the ladies," observed Isadora. "I hear who took advantage of the girls."

"Whoever did for him deserves a prize," said Betty following the script that she and Izzy had planned out.

"How well did you know him?" asked Isadora as she reached over to take Kathy's empty glass and refilled it with her flask.

"Too well," replied Kathy. "he used to take me out. Promised me that we had a future. Used me and then laughed at me when he said he was going to marry a classy broad from his own social class. He said I was only good for one thing, but we could still get together after he was married. So, I poisoned his flask. He'll never laugh at me again.

"That's terrible," said Izzy feeling sorry for her despite the fact that she murdered Wicker.

"That is terrible," said Sergeant Starkey as he jumped out from behind the screen. But it's still murder. "Katy Smith, if that's your real name, you are under arrest or the murder of Ronald Anthony Wicker." He signaled to two men sitting at a nearby table, who happened to be policemen. The got up and escorted Katy Smith out of the dining room.

"Got anything left in that flask?" Jeff asked Izzy. She passed it to him and he took a drink.

"What's going to happen to her?" asked Betty.

"My guess is," he answered, "that a good lawyer will plead temporary insanity. She'll spend the next ten years or so in a mental hospital."

"That's awful," sighed Isadora.

"Better that then life in prison. Now I better get down to the police station and get her booked." He got up and turned to the two ladies. "Good job, you two."

Isadora wanted to be the one to break the news to the Wickers, so as soon as Kathy Smith was arrested, she headed to the Wicker's home on Washington Street. As she rang the bell she was curious as to how the Wickers would react to the news.

The maid who answered the door recognized her from her previous visit. "Come in Miss Drake," she said holding the door open for her, "I'll see if the family is home."

"Thank you..." Isadora tried to come up with a name and it took her a few seconds to search her memory, "Jane."

"I don't know if you remember, but I was ahead of you in high school."

"Ah! Jane Grant! Class of..."

Jane held up her hand. "Don't remind me."

"Who is it Jane?" came a woman's voice from another room."

"It's Miss Drake."

"Well, sent her in, and go tell Mr. Wicker to come to the drawing room."

"Miss Drake, would you like some tea?"

"Yes, thank you."

"Mr. Wicker should be here shortly." Mrs. Wicker rang for tea and before she could count to ten a maid appeared with a tea set.

Mr. Wicker entered the room as Mrs. Wicker poured the tea. "Good afternoon, Mis Drake. What brings you here?" he asked as he took the cup of tea that his wife offered.

"I thought you should be the first to know that Ronnie's killer has been arrested."

"Are you sure?" asked Mrs. Wicker with tears in her eyes.

"Yes, I'm sure. I was there." Isadora went on to give a full account of the events.

"So, it was really you who solved the case," said Mr. Wicker clearly impressed.

"With a lot of help," she replied modestly."

"Don't be so modest. Now if you ladies will excuse me a moment I'll be right back." Mr. Wicker jumped up and headed out of the room. He returned and passed an envelope to Isadora. She opened it and saw a check for a hundred dollars.

"But the Brocktons have already paid me for

the case," she protested.

"This isn't payment," said Mr. Wicker. "This is a retainer. I'd like you to look into something for me."

"I see," replied Isadora not really seeing at all.

"My cousin, Jasper Chamberlain, established an investment business. Last week he committed suicide. At least that's what the police investigators believe. I don't believe it for a minute. I'd like you to look into it."

"But if the police think it was suicide…"

He interrupted her. "I don't think for a minute that he killed himself and I have reason to believe that he was murdered."

"Very well." Isadora reached into her handbag and pulled out a note book. "Tell me all about it."

Mr. Wicker sat back and took a deep breath. "Jasper and I grew up together. We both attended the University of Maine. Jasper studied economics and went on to establish an investment firm Chamberlain and Bracket. He and Mr. Bracket made a successful business from the time they opened, and I don't have to tell you how the stock market is booming these days."

"I understand that even bus boys are buying stock."

"Yes, so anyway he had no reason to despair of his business. In his personal life he had been a widower these last ten years, so it's unlikely that he killed himself over grief."

Isadora opened her mouth to speak but he held up his hand. "He had just got engaged to a lovey widow, and he said he had found happiness once again."

"What is her name?" Isadora asked poised to write it down in her notebook.

"She's Mrs. Andrew Webber; that is Lillian Webber." He gave Isadora her address.

"Why do the police think it's suicide?"

"He had attempted suicide once right after his wife died."

"There is more to the story," said Mrs. Wicker who had been silent during the recitation. "he was found with a suicide note and a gun in his hand."

"Then you do not share Mr. Wicker's belief that it was murder?" asked Isadora.

"I do not. The evidence is overwhelming," said Mrs. Wicker giving her husband a look of defiance.

"And Mr. Wicker what evidence do you have that Mr. Chamberlain was murdered?"

"Jasper was left-handed, yet he was found with a gun in his right hand."

Isadora wasn't sure that was evidence enough, yet something told her to take the case. "Very well," she said, "I'll see what I can find out."

"Thank you, Miss Drake," said Mr. Wicker. "If you need more money for expenses please let me know."

"I think this will be more than enough to start with."

Sergeant Jeff Starkey looked up from his desk where he was doing paperwork only to see Isadora Drake standing in front of his desk. "Izzy, what can I do for you?"

"I'm interested in the case of Jasper Chamberlain." Uninvited she took a seat in the chair in front of his desk.

"Chamberlain? Ah yes, the suicide. What about it?"

"His cousin, Mr. Wicker, believes that he was murdered. He's hired me to look into it."

"He's wasting your time and his money. The gun was in his hand and a suicide note was on his desk," sighed Jeff. "Case closed."

"Well, Jeff, thank you for your time. You've been a big help." The sarcasm wasn't lost on Jeff. "I'll be going."

"Would you like to see the suicide note?" Jeff asked as she was about to leave.

"Yes, I would, thank you." Jeff noted there was no sarcasm in her voice this time.

Jeff got up and went to one of the file cabinets. Isadora watched him with appreciation. He was so handsome. Too bad he was…"

"Here it is," said Jeff passing the note to her and cutting off her line of thought,

Isadora gingerly took the note and read it. Something, she thought, was not quite right about the note. "Did you check it for fingerprints?"

"There wasn't any," he said.

"So you're telling me that Chamberlain wiped his prints off the note before he shot himself?"

"This was not my case," said Jeff when he realized that was indeed strange.

"And why," asked Isadora, "does it look like the top of the note was cut off? And it appears to have been cut off where the date should be?"

"Why indeed?" echoed Jeff who was surprised at Isadora's keen eye. "But the case is closed and it's not my case so I can't reopen it.

"Maybe you can't," smiled Isadora, "but I can."

"Heaven help us," muttered Jeff as he watched Isadora walk away."

Dr. Bushy Miller entered his office and noticed that both his receptionist and his nurse had already arrived and were having their coffee. "Good morning Miss Drake and Mrs. Welby."

"Good morning Dr. Miller," the two said in unison.

"I'll get you a cup of coffee," offered Judy Welby.

"Thank you."

"Where's Flora this morning?" asked Isadora.

"She's helping your brother set up his shop."

'Something is up with those two," stated Izzy.

"No doubt about it."

"No doubt about what?" asked Judy Welby as she entered the reception area with Bushy's steaming cup of coffee.

"Our siblings seem to be dating," explained Izzy.

"How delicious!" she exclaimed. Both Bushy and Isadora had figured out that Mrs. Welby loved gossip.

"What's on the schedule today?" Bushy asked Izzy, mostly to change the subject.

"You have no appointments until eleven o'clock. I've put some files on your desk for you to review," Isadora explained.

Bushy headed into his office as the phone rang. She answered the ring and turned pale as she listened to the other end of the phone. She put the phone down and ran for the doctor's office.

"Bushy!" she yelled forgetting office decorum. "It's my granny. She has taken a fall in the house."

"I'll get my bag," said Bushy.

"I'm going with you," Isadora grabbed her hand bag.

"Of course. Mrs. Welby would you look after the office?"

"Yes, no problem. I hope your grandmother will be okay."

"I hope so, too," replied Izzy as she followed Bushy out to his automobile.

Chapter 20

"Ow!" said Rose as Bushy Miller checked her shoulder. She was sitting on the sofa and looking miserable.

"What did you do?" asked Isadora quite concerned.

"I missed the bottom step as I was coming down the stairs."

"You've hurt your back rather badly," Bushy informed the two of them. "But nothing is broken. Take some aspirin powders and keep your activities to a minimum. It seems your family is accident prone," he added referring to Isadora's recent injury on the church steps.

"But I'm supposed to go out dancing tonight," Rose protested.

"You are not going dancing or any other foolishness," said Bushy in a forceful voice. "And you need to stay in bed for a few days. Maybe in a week you will feel better. I'll get you a cane to use in the meantime."

"Only old people need canes," Rose said to the doctor.

"Exactly."

Rose uttered a word so rude that even Isadora was shocked. "Granny!" Isadora had never heard that word from her grandmother. In fact, she had only heard it one other time when Anna was instructing her on swear words. Bushy threw back his head and laughed so hard he had tears in his eyes.

"I'm glad I'm providing you with amusement." Rose muttered in a sulky voice.

"I'll send my nurse over to check on you periodically. I need to get back to the office for an appointment. Now is there anything you need?"

"I'm quite capable of taking care of myself."

"I will stay with her until Mrs. Welby gets here," offered Isadora.

"That's a good idea," responded Bushy.

Peter Drake was Busy installing a speaker box on the outside of his radio shop. He had the idea of broadcasting radio programs for any passersby. It was good advertising and would make people want to have their own radio sets at home. Next, he would have to get up on the roof and string a long wire antenna. As well as radios he would sell the parts for antennas. Not everyone could have an outside aerial so he would stock some of those compact wire antennas that would sit on top of the radio cabinet. They would be almost as good as the long wire aerials.

Meanwhile Flora Miller was inside unpacking the latest arrivals and setting up an accounting system for the store. She had never seen so many radios and so many different styles and prices. She thought the inventory was too large for the Bath market. Maine had fifteen radio broadcast stations in 1921, but was that enough variety for listeners?

Peter was so excited about his new shop that Flora kept her doubts to herself. In the window she placed a sign that said Grand Opening Soon.

Bushy Miller ran his fingers through his thick curly hair and checked his reflection in the mirror. He had sent Nurse Welby to look after Rose Garland and was glad to have some alone time with Izzy. It seemed that both he and Isadora had been too busy lately to have any time together.

Izzy, for her part had gone to her closet and changed before returning to the office. She, too, was eager to return to the office where she would be alone with Bushy. He probably would be too busy with patients to notice, but as she thought nothing lost, nothing gained.

They both had realized what a gossip his new nurse was and so they had to be formal with each other in her presence. She just hoped her grandmother wouldn't mention anything about Bushy and herself, but she sighed knowing her grandmother loved gossip as well.

"You look dazzling," Bushy said as Izzy walked through the door wearing a flowered dress tailored in the latest fashion.

"And you look dashing as ever," she responded. "No patients?"

"Not for another hour," he said with a wicked smile. "Come here."

She went up to him and he took her in his arms and kissed her. Izzy felt like she was on fire and her knees were like rubber. This was a new feeling for her, and she thought that she might possibly like it. She moved her hands and ran them over Bushy's well-developed chest. The fire she felt before now felt like she was in a furnace, and then the phone rang.

"Don't answer it," whispered Bushy. But they both knew the moment was over.

"It could be an emergency," she whispered back. He released her and she ran to the phone. "You better come in," she said to the person on the telephone. She hung up. "That was Mrs. Lovejoy. She says she's having heart palpitations."

"I've told her to cut down on the coffee."

"She'll be here in five minutes. I suspect," Izzy said with a grin, "that the palpitations are caused by the idea of seeing her handsome new doctor." It was well known that widow Lovejoy liked the men.

Rose Garland sat on her sofa with her feet up on a footstool. She and Judy Welby were having a glass of sherry together. "Miss Drake and Dr. Miller seem like a nice couple," commented Mrs. Welby.

"Yes," agreed Rose, "almost like they are

brother and sister, or employer and employee." Rose knew that Judy was pumping her for information. She knew herself how to get information from people. "Why have you seen anything going on?"

Nurse Welby wasn't a liar, so she had to admit the truth. "No, nothing. It just seems that a good-looking man and a good-looking woman would be attracted to each other."

"I don't think Dr. Miller is the marrying type," added Rose who was enjoying fueling speculation in her unwitting visitor."

"You mean…"

"Well, he doesn't seem interested in women." Let her think about that Rose thought to herself.

Isadora checked the address of the house on High Street against the address in her notebook. Lillian Webber, the fiancé of Jasper Chamberlain, might have some insight about Chamberlain's suicide. While High Street was not as fashionable as Washington Street, the houses, nonetheless, were imposing. She walked up to the door noticing the blooming flower beds on either side of the entrance.

The doorbell was answered by a fiftyish woman in a black, but fashionable dress. Before the woman could say anything, Isadora handed her a business card. "Inquiries?" said the woman as she read Isadora's business card. "What are you inquiring about?"

"I'm inquiring about Jasper Chamberlain's suicide."

"You better come in, then," said the woman who had suddenly turned pale. "I'm Lillian Webber," she said introducing herself. "Please have a seat." The parlor was a formal room that was furnished in the latest style. Isadora wasn't sure she liked the room.

"I'm representing a client who believes that Mr. Chamberlain was murdered, that he didn't commit suicide."

"As you probably know he and I were engaged. I, too, believe it wasn't suicide. And I might add neither does his daughter."

"Daughter?" This was news to Isadora. "Mr. Wicker had mentioned no daughter."

"Yes, Millie Sotheby. Mr. Sotheby is a rather wealthy business man. Millie was very close to her father."

"Do you have her address?" Isadora wrote down the address. Still mystified as to why Mr. Wicker had not mentioned her.

"How can I help?" Lillian asked.

"Can you think of any reason why Mr. Chamberlain would kill himself?"

"None at all. He was looking to the future and planning out his life." Isadora noticed the tears in her eyes.

"When was the last time you saw him?" Isadora asked.

"The day before he died. We were having dinner at the hotel. It would have been inappropriate for him to come here."

"Did he seem worried about anything that you noticed?"

"No, he was very happy and light of heart."

"Did he have any enemies that you know of?" Isadora was beginning to have her doubts about the suicide herself.

"Not that I know of," Lillian answered. "Everyone seemed to like Jasper."

"The evidence of suicide is overwhelming," Isadora wanted to see how she would react to that. "He was found with a gun in his hand and a suicide note. It has been confirmed that it was in his own handwriting."

"I can't explain it," said Lillian, "but I know it wasn't suicide."

As Isadora left the house, she wondered why two persons he was close to believed it was murder, despite the evidence.

Despite the fact that Peter's radio shop had not yet opened, a crowd had gathered in front of the shop. They were listening to the radio speaker that Peter had installed outside, and Peter knew he had chosen the best way to advertise the wonders of radio.

He and Flora had come up with a sales plan. Peter would be the salesman explaining all the technological features of the radio. Flora would give customers a lesson on how to operate the radio before a buyer left the shop. Peter had hired a friend from Edison's workshop who would be able to fix any problems with the radios. Jack Evans would arrive tomorrow in time for the opening of the shop. He felt people would be more interested in purchasing a radio if they knew that they could, if needed, get their machine repaired. Radios were not cheap and people needed to think about the payoff for their investments.

Flora had suggested the new sales scheme of offering payments on time. He was beginning to think that Flora was a good business manager.

Isadora sat at her desk and was having her morning coffee with Flora and Nurse Welby. "What time is the store opening?" Judy Welby asked.

"We'll be opening at noon," she answered. It was Saturday and many people worked five and a half days. Most people went shopping on Saturday afternoon in Bath.

"Your brother and I will be there of course," Isadora told her.

"Me, too," said Mrs. Welby. "My husband is really interested in radio."

"So we'll get to meet Mr. Welby?" asked Isadora.

"Yes, indeed," she answered.

"I should be going," Flora explained. "I need to get ready for the opening."

"Good morning everyone," greeted Bushy as

he entered the office. "Coffee!" Mrs. Welby rushed off to pour Bushy a cup of the liquid brew.

"Bushy," said Flora. "I'll see you at the store later."

"We'll be there."

Isadora was pleased that Bushy used 'we' instead of 'I.' But did it mean anything?"

"What's on the schedule today?" asked Bushy who rarely made his own appointments.

"You're needed for a house call. Mrs. Baker's two sons have the chicken pox."

"There isn't much I can do for chicken pox," sighed Bushy. "Except tell her to use ointment and give them aspirin powder.

Chapter 21

A crowd of about a dozen potential radio fans were gathered outside Drake's Radio Emporium. The store was due to open in a few minutes. Inside Peter Drake and Flora Miller were getting ready to open. Visiting to help celebrate the opening were Isadora and Bushy. Flora was finishing a sign offering a ten percent discount on any radios sold on opening day. She placed it in the window and heard reaction from the crowd.

Isadora and Flora had decorated the store with colorful festoons. Granny Rose enter the store from the back and came in hobbling on her new cane. Peter called for attention and the group gathered in silence. "I have an announcement, Peter spoke with some excitement, "Thank you all for helping out. This is a day for two celebrations: the new opening of the store, and the good news that Flora has agreed to marry me,"

There was stunned silence for a moment and then the sound of congratulations for the couple. Isadora ran up to Flora, "I'm so excited," she gushed and gave her a hug. "We'll be sisters!"

Rose and Bushy looked at each other sharing

the thought that they were too young. Both knew better than to express their doubts, because it really wasn't any of their business.

When the doors finally opened the crowd rushed in and by the end of the first day Peter had sold four expensive radios along with two crystal sets. He and Flora estimated that they only had to sell three radios a week to keep afloat

Isadora and Anna Greyson sat in the corner of the Speak checking out the crowd. "Who does she think she is?" asked Anna about the bottle blonde in the gold dress that was two sizes smaller than the subject of their conversation.

"I'd say that's her working clothes," speculated Isadora as she took a sip of the sidecar that was hiding in her coffee cup.

"I don't think I'd want that job."

"We're only seeing the back of her," added Anna, "When she turns around, I'll bet she's ugly."

"Not likely and she was flirting with Mr. Wilcox, who by the way, is married."

"There is something familiar about her," observed Anna.

"How can you tell from the back?"

"I don't know, but there is."

"She's leaving with Wilcox," said Isadora as they watched her head to the door on the arm of Mr. Wilcox. At the door the blonde turned around for a moment and then waved to Izzy and Anna and made a stabbing motion with her arm. "It can't be her!"

"I don't believe it!" Anna said shocked to the core.

"She had us all fooled!" said Izzy in shock.

"To think," added the shocked Anna, "that Mary Brocton is a floozy."

"I have a feeling that Mary Brocton is more than a floozy. In fact, virgin Mary Brocton may not be a virgin at all."

Billy Brown spotted Isadora and Anna at the Speak and joined them at their table. "You'll never guess what we just saw." Anna was only too happy to inform Billy about the floozy blonde.

"I don't believe it," stated Billy. "First off Mary is not a blonde. She has that mousey brown hair. And her religious activities are too intense to be an act."

"I'm telling you that was Mary Brocton," Isadora said firmly. "And as for the blonde hair it was probably a wig."

"Here comes your boyfriend," Anna informed Billy as Sergeant Jeff Starkey entered the Speak. He was wearing a hat and glasses in an attempt not to be recognized.

"Nice outfit," said Isadora as Jeff joined them.

"It's an attempt to be incognito," Jeff informed her. "It wouldn't do to be recognized as a policeman. Everyone would think it was a raid. Policemen like a drink now and then you know."

"I'm sure they do," added Billy who looked at

Jeff. "I know you do. You'll never guess what these two flappers told me."

"I'm sure I'll never guess," Jeff looked at the two ladies.

"Mary Brocton was here at the Speak dressed in a Blonde wig and a tight dress and left with a married man," Anna informed Jeff.

Jeff laughed, "You're looney."

"You should check her out," Isadora told Jeff.

"Why? Even if it was her there is nothing illegal about what she did. You think you're a detective. You go and detect."

"I am a detective as you well know, and I will look into it."

"Speaking of being a detective," said Billy. "How is your suicide case proceeding?"

"I don't know. Mr. Wicker is convinced it was murder. And his fiancé also believes that it wasn't suicide. Yet all the evidence suggests suicide." Isadora looked puzzled.

"So, what's your next step?" Billy asked.

"I'll go interview the daughter and the business partner."

"If it is murder," suggested Jeff, "look for a motive. It's either money, love, or hate."

"But you believe it was suicide," challenged Isadora.

"I do," responded Jeff. "I think if you investigate, you'll come to believe it too."

"We'll see."

"Sorry I'm late," said Bushy as he sat down. No

one saw him enter. "I had an emergency to attend to. What did I miss?"

Isadora gave him a brief version of their conversation. "You must be kidding," said Bushy as he signaled for a drink.

Isadora didn't sleep that night. There was too much on her mind. She had to investigate a suicide and she had no idea how to disprove the idea of suicide, but what really bothered her was Mary Brocton. How could an innocent, church-going girl like her, turn up at the Speak with a married man? She was determined to find out. And, of course, what was up with Jeff Starkey and Billie Brown? She had a good idea about that one, but she wanted conformation. Not that she cared about that. In fact she rather liked the idea that Billie had a special friend. And then what about Bushy Miller? Was he really interested in her?

She must have dozed off because she was startled when the alarm clock went off. She freshened up, grabbed her bathrobe, and headed to the kitchen. "Coffee!" she gasped.

"Well, you look like a sight this morning," said Rose as she poured a cup from the coffee pot and passed it to Isadora.

"I had a bad night," she answered between gulps of coffee.

"I don't doubt it. You're too busy. You need to relax and enjoy life."

"I enjoy life," Izzy defended herself. But she

had some doubt.

Rose's housekeeper, Mrs. Baker, came in the backdoor, hung up her coat and hat, and began preparing breakfast. "It's going to be a hot one," she said as a greeting.

"Then I better dress for it," sighed Izzy. "The office is so hot in the afternoon."

"Eat something first," scolded Mrs. Baker, who believed a good breakfast was the key to happiness.

Flora had made coffee at the office when Isadora entered to start the day. It was her third cup that morning and Izzy wasn't sure if that would be enough. "Good morning ladies," said Bushy as he entered the room.

"Good morning, doctor," said Flora and Izzy at the same time.

"We've got a busy day, today," Bushy said brightly.

Isadora groaned, "Can't wait."

The phone rang and Isadora took the call. "It's Nurse Welby," Isadora said as she hung up the phone. "Her husband is ill and she's taking the day off."

"Then I'll need you to assist me in the exam room when we have a female patient."

"But I don't know anything about being a nurse," she protested.

"You just need to be present to preserve propriety."

"Fine, but no blood."

The first patient was a young married woman. Isadora had to avert her eyes as he examined her. She had little stomach for intimate exams. She hoped the next patient was a man, so she could escape the exam room. Mrs. Freemont, as the young woman was named, wanted information about birth control. Isadora's eyes opened wide has Bushy explained the various methods. She was shocked at what she heard. She would have to talk to Anna. She figured Anna might know more about it.

The next three patients were men as she got to return to the reception desk and breathed a sigh of relief.

Isadora stood outside the home of the Brocton's and considered if she was on a fool's mission or not. She walked up to the door and took the large door knocker in her hand and knocked on the door. "I'm here to see Miss Brocton," she said as the maid opened the door.

"Miss Brocton is in her room. I'll take you up." Isadora followed the maid up the stairs and down the long hallway. "Miss Drake is here to see you," the maid informed Mary and then left the room.

"Izzy, this is a surprise," Mary said. "Have a seat."

Isadora looked around the room, or as she observed, the suite. Isadora took a seat in the sitting area in a large chintz covered chair across from

Mary.

"I'll get right to the point. I saw you at the Speak with Mr. Wilcox. I have to tell you you're playing with fire."

"What are you talking about?" Mary looked confused.

"I'm talking about you acting like a floozy."

"Have you lost your mind?" Mary seemed shocked and upset.

Isadora didn't like the way that Mary looked. She got up, crossed to what was Mary's closet, and searched until she found the gold dress hidden in the back of the closet. She pulled it out and confronted Mary with the evidence. "And just what is this?" To her shock Mary began to cry,

"Oh, Izzy," she said sobbing, "strange things keep happening to me. I've never seen that dress before. And I found this under my bed, I don't even know what it is." She handed Izzy a small round case made of celluloid.

Izzy carefully opened the case. It took her a moment to figure it out as she picked the rubber object out of the case. Having just sat through Bushy's instructions about birth control with Mrs. Freeman, she had a good idea what it was. "And you've never seen it before?"

"No, never! Oh, Izzy, what's happening?"

Izzy hugged her, "I don't know, but I'm going to find out."

It was a perfect night for a walk. It wasn't hot

and it wasn't cool, and a slight breeze kept the bugs away. Isadora picked up Anna and they drove down to Popham Beach to walk along the ocean. They parked near the unfinished stone fort, took off their shoes and walked in the surf. The glow of the little one-celled sea creatures looked like fireflies in the water.

"She must be lying," said Anna as Izzy related her visit with Mary Brocton. "We saw her and she saw us.

"I thought so at first, but she seemed too distressed when I confronted her. Of course, it could be an act."

"She was probably scared that her parents might find out."

"She should be. Apparently, she's been sleeping with Wilcox, or at least she's using birth control."

"How do you know that?"

"There was a diaphragm hidden in her room."

"How do you know about diaphragms?" Anna asked.

"I had to sit through a conversation Bushy had about birth control with a patient,"

"What did you think about it?" Anna was curious.

"I think it's messy and way too much work to be worth it," she said.

Anna just shook her head. "Oh, Honey, it's more than worth it."

Chapter 22

I sadora Drake realized that she had to organize her time. Lately it seemed she was flying from one thing to the other. It was time to slow down, and as her grandmother told her, she needed to enjoy life. She would set one task at a time, and leave some time for a social life. But she was stumped. How do you enjoy life when there is so much to do?

"You look lost in thought, Miss Drake," said Dr. Miller as he came out of his office for a cup of coffee.

"I'm trying to organize my life."

"If you are free for dinner tonight, I might be able to help you." He looked around to make sure Nurse Welby was out of hearing range. He put his hand on her shoulder, and she thought for a moment she would melt into the floor. "I'll pick you up at seven."

"I'll be ready," she said forgetting to breathe for a second."

"There you are, Dr. Miller," said Nurse Welby as she came out of the storage room with an armload of medical supplies.

"Let me help you," he said as he took the supplies from her and headed into the office.

"That's one good looking man," said Mrs. Welby as she watched him retreat into the exam room.

"You think so?" asked Izzy feigning disinterest.

"You're hopeless," Nurse Welby replied and just shook her head.

Izzy snuggled up to Bushy in the seat of his old Ford. To her surprise he was driving away from town. "Where are we going?" she asked, but didn't really car.

"I thought we might have a nice dinner at the inn in Freeport. They have excellent food and you are dressed to be seen."

"Thank you, it's just an ordinary dress." She had actually stopped off at Betty's Dress Shop and picked out a peach colored dress that complimented her red-auburn hair. It was daring with its low-cut top and mid knee length.

"There's nothing ordinary about that dress." He noticed that she had defied the flat look fashion and accented her curves to advantage. "And if I wasn't driving, I'd kiss you." He pulled the car over to the side of the road, took her in his arms and kissed her. He put his hand on her leg, and she had no will-power to stop him. And then the engine died.

"Damnation!" he swore and hopped out of the

car, went to the rear of the car, lifted up the top of the trunk, took out the crank. He carefully inserted the crank into the engine and attempted to start the car. He needed to be careful. He had doctored several broken arms that had been broken when the patient had forgotten to take their hand off the crank. The car started on the third attempt and roared into life. He climbed in, adjusted the timing, and off they went.

"I think it's time I get a new car," he said as they headed down the road.

"As a doctor you need to have a reliable car." They both spoke in formal sentences trying so as not to talk about their little scene.

Suddenly Bushy broke out laughing, "I wonder what would have happened if the car hadn't stalled."

"I've no idea," she responded, "but I think we both would have enjoyed it."

The restaurant at the inn practically screamed Maine. It was paneled in weathered wood and on one wall was back woods fishing gear artfully arranged, and on the other wall, were lobster traps and colorful lobster buoys. Bushy held the chair for her and the waiter rushed over with their menus. "Would you like a cup of our special tea?" he asked.

"How special?" asked Bushy.

"Gin and tonic," the waiter whispered.

"Bring us two," Bushy ordered. In a short

amount of time the waiter brought over two very large coffee cups and took their order.

"I can tell something is on your mind, Izzy. Tell big bad Bushy all about it."

"Hmm, big and bad. I like that." She went on to tell him about her visit with Mary Brocton.

"She must be lying." Bushy was as confused as Izzy.

"I don't think so. She was genuinely distressed. If you had seen her like that, you'd believe she was innocent too."

"What about the stabbing motion she made to you and Anna?" Bushy asked.

"Well," Izzy hesitated, "I think she may have been the one to stab Ronnie Wicker, though his best friend swears he accidently stabbed himself."

"Try to encourage her to come as see me," suggested Bushy. "She might need some medical attention."

"You think so?"

"It's a start," he said as the waiter brought their meals and set it before them.

Rose was waiting up for Izzy. "How was your date with the handsome doctor?" she asked before Izzy was even through the front door.

"It was fine," she answered turning beet red.

"By the look on your face it was more than fine."

"Granny, what am I going to do? I think I'm in love with him."

"I think he's in love with you, too."

"I hope so. When he kisses me I just want to melt."

"Ah, that takes me back. I've melted a few times myself, well maybe more than a few times. Bring him over for lunch tomorrow. Then excuse yourself for a few minutes. I'm going to ask him what his intentions are toward you."

"What if he doesn't have any?" Izzy had a worried look on her face.

"Believe me girl, he's got intentions."

Chapter 23

J ack Evans, the radio repair guy who Peter Drake hired, sat in his little repair room and was making a list of parts and tubes so he could be ready for any repairs. Most radio problems boiled down to burned out tubes. Once he had his list, he filled out the order forms and put them in the mail. With nothing to do until the parts came in he began building crystal sets. These little inexpensive radios need no electricity and were good for those living in the more distant parts of Bath which had no electric service. Peter had said that they were a hook to get others interested in more advanced radios. The more advanced radios could be powered with batteries or city power.

Peter and Jack had been friends since they started working for Edison back in 1919. "I have an idea," he said to Peter and Flora as the three of them had lunch in the back room.

"What is it?" asked Peter. Flora had noted that the two of them rarely talked in complex sentences. She figured they had work together for so long, they could communicate with each other using few words. In fact, she was beginning to think that men were very different than women.

"I think you should consider adding phonographs to your inventory. Why not be a seller of all types of entertainment?"

"And phonograph records as well," added Flora.

"I like the idea," Peter responded after a few minutes of thought. "Since radio repairs won't be needed with new radios for a while, I'll put you in charge of the phonographs and records. That will give you something to do until the repairs begin to come in."

"I'd like that. So much better that working for you know who."

"Yes, Edison's laboratory was frantic most of the time."

Bushy pushed back his chair from the table. "That was a very fine lunch, Mrs. Garland."

"Thank you. I'll let Mrs. Baker know," said Rose. "And we'll have coffee and dessert. Izzy, would you go to the kitchen and help Mrs. Baker with dessert?"

"Yes, of course," said Izzy. She wished she could listen at the door to hear what Bushy would say to Rose. But maybe she really didn't want to know.

"Young man," said Rose getting right to the point, "what are your intentions about my grand-daughter?"

"I'm in love with her, Mrs. Garland," he sighed. "But I don't know how she feels."

"I want to take both of you and shake you until your teeth rattle. Are you blind? She's in love with you."

"She is?" Bushy wanted to get up and dance.

Rose reach over and swatted him on the head. "Dolt!" she said. "And are your intentions honorable?"

"Ah, sure," he said taken by surprise.

"That's what I thought," she said. "Until I see an engagement ring on her finger you are not to sleep with her. Do you understand?"

"Yes, ma'am."

"Here's coffee," announced Isadora as she came into the dining room. "Mrs. Baker will bring in a nice chocolate cake she's made. Bushy, what's the matter? You're bright red!"

"He had a little coughing fit while you were in the kitchen," Rose explained quickly. As soon as Bushy wasn't looking Rose gave Izzy a signal that all is well.

"Ah, here's the chocolate cake," said Bushy to change the subject.

The screaming from the Brown household could be heard out on the street. "You are a disgrace, a failure, and a pervert!" yelled Billy's father. "I had to hear about you from my co-workers. Can you imagine how humiliated I was?"

"I am none of those things!" Billy yelled back.

"And as of this moment, I have no father!" Billie picked up his bag and left the house, much to the shock of his father.

"Billy," yelled his mother to his retreating back. "Come back!"

Billy swung his body around. "And you let him hit me and said nothing. I now consider myself an orphan."

"See what you've done!" yelled Mrs. Brown in tears as she walked past her husband and gave him a shove for all she was worth. "I hope you're happy." And she stalked away.

No, thought Mr. Brown. I'm not happy at all.

Millie Sotheby answered the door of the big brick house. "Mrs. Sotheby?" asked Isadora. It was obvious that she wasn't a maid by the expensive dress she was wearing.

"Yes, what do you want?" she asked wondering why this young woman was standing on her front steps.

"I'm Isadora Drake," answered Izzy as she handed her card to the woman. "I'm here about Mr. Chamberlain's suicide."

"He did not commit suicide," Millie Sotheby told her with an icy voice.

"I'm here to prove that he didn't commit suicide," Isadora stated.

"Come in, then," Mrs. Sotheby seemed relieved.

Izzy was taken into a large room that was

sparsely furnished at least compared to the overfilled Victorian rooms of which she had seen too many. The furniture was expensive solid wood and looked like they were one of a kind. "Please have a seat, Miss Drake."

"Thank you. My client believes that Mr. Chamberlain was murdered as does his former fiancé."

"With good reason."

"All the evidence points to suicide. What makes you think it was murder?"

"He had no reason to commit suicide. His business was doing well and he was happily engaged."

"But he had tried to commit suicide once before."

"My mother had just died and he was beside himself with grief. He bought a gun and wrote a suicide note. But the point is that even then, at the lowest point of his life, he couldn't bring himself to do it."

"You do make a point, Mrs. Sotheby. Who inherits his estate?"

"Mr. Brackett receives the business, and I receive the rest. Though some money was put aside for his future wife."

"But if he remarried, wouldn't she receive most of it," Isadora was fishing since she had no other facts to go on.

"If you are suggesting that I'm interested in his money, look around. My husband is wealthy.

Probably more than my father ever was."

"Did he have any enemies?"

"Not that I'm aware of. He was a fair man in business, and people seemed to like him."

"Thank you for your time," said Isadora getting up to go. "If you think of anything, anything at all, give me a call."

"I will. And good luck. I hope you find something."

Chapter 24

Something was wrong with Billy Brown, thought Isadora as she walked into the Kennebec Diner to meet Jeff Starkey. She wasn't sure why Billy was there. "Good morning gentlemen," she said as both men stood up until she was seated.

The two men greeted her and it was then that she saw that Billy had a suitcase with him. "Why do you have a suitcase, Billy? Are you taking a trip?"

"His father kicked him out of the house," explained Jeff.

"Oh, dear! Where will you go?" she asked and then realized he might have nowhere to go.

"Bushy said he has plenty of room in his house. I'm going to stay there."

Isadora gave Jeff a look. "He can't stay with me," explained Jeff. "We have to be discrete."

"That's unfair," remarked Isadora. "It's nobody's business."

"That's true," said Jeff. "But this is real life."

"Jeff is thinking of having a house built," explained Billy. "It's going to look like two houses with one entrance facing one street, and the other facing another street. That way we have two different addresses. And inside will be one big house." Billy actually sounded excited.

"Wouldn't it be easier to go to a big city where you can be anonymous and people don't care what their neighbors do?" she asked. A waitress came over and gave Isadora a cup of coffee.

"That's one option," Jeff added.

"Anyway, what I came to tell you," Izzy said to Jeff, "is that I met with Chamberlain's daughter who is also convinced that his death was not a suicide."

"And did she give you any solid evidence?"

"No, but she feels…"

"Feelings aren't evidence," Jeff shook his head.

"The suicide note is still in evidence, isn't it?" she asked.

"Yes, it is. But Chamberlain's hand writing has already been verified. He wrote that suicide note."

"I want to look at it again," she insisted.

"Stop by the office, but it's genuine," said Jeff.

"I'm sure it is," she responded. He opened his mouth to say something, but changed his mind. "Well, I better get to work," she told them. "Billy, why don't you come with me and get set up at Bushy's house?"

He picked up his suitcase and followed her out the door.

Nurse Welby and Flora were already in the office having their morning coffee when Isadora entered after getting Billy settled. She picked up an empty cup and poured out some coffee. "I'll go make another pot," said Judy Welby as she headed off to the kitchen.

"How's my brother's store coming along?" she asked Flora.

"Better than expected. We're going to add phonographs and recordings."

Isadora notice that Flora said 'we'. "What happens when everyone has a radio?"

"Then they will want to have one for each room. And as prices come down people will want better and newer models. And records will always be in demand."

Dr. Miller entered the office ready to start the day. "What do we have this morning, Miss Drake?"

"I've managed to convince Mary Brocton to come in to see you."

"Then I'll have Mrs. Welby cover the office, and I'd like you to be with me in the exam room. She'll feel more comfortable with you there."

"What are you going to do when she gets here?" asked Izzy.

"I'm not sure. We'll have to make it up as we go along."

"Wonderful," she said with full on irony.

When Mary Brocton appeared at the office she was dressed modestly and said she had just come from morning mass. Her hair was pulled back and hidden under her hat. The only jewelry she had on was a rather large silver crucifix around her neck. She had a missal in her hand and looked every inch a devote young lady.

"Good morning everyone," Mary said cheerfully. "It's a wonderful morning. Izzy suggested that I should come to see you."

"I understand that there is some confusion in your life," Bushy answered.

"I think someone is playing tricks on me."

"Let's start with a physical exam. Nurse Welby will take you to the exam room and get you ready."

The exam tested her reflexes, her heart rate, and her lungs were clear. He checked her eye movements and her teeth. She answered his questions as the exam continued. "Am I okay, Dr. Miller?"

"You are as healthy as you should be. Get dressed and we'll have a little talk in my office. I'll send Miss Drake in to be with you."

Dr. Miller sat behind his desk while Izzy and Mary sat in two chairs facing him. He thought sitting at the desk would give Mary confidence that he was a professional who could help her. "Miss Drake has filled me in on some of the situation you are going through. Why don't you tell me in your own words."

"I don't know where to start," Mary looked thoughtful.

"Start at the beginning. Leave nothing out. Even a small detail might be helpful."

"It all started when my parents forced me to accept Ronnie Wicker's marriage proposal."

"You didn't like him?" asked Bushy.

"I liked him well enough. He was handsome and good looking, and had a good sense of humor. But I also knew that he was being forced to marry me. And I didn't want an arranged marriage. And Ronnie was, how shall I say, not morally upright if you know what I mean. On our first date he picked me up in his car, but I don't remember anything after that. The next day I woke up with a headache and as the maid was picking up my clothes, she asked me how my dress got so soiled."

Izzy and Bushy shared a look. "How was it soiled?" asked Izzy.

"The back of the dress had dirt and pine needles all over it. When I asked Ronnie, he said I had fallen on the ground, but I don't remember anything," she wailed.

Izzy got up and fetched her a glass of water. When Mary had calmed down Izzy asked her how much she had had to drink.

"I don't drink," she answered.

"What about the gold dress that Izzy found in your closet?" Bushy asked.

To their shock, Mary began to laugh hysterically.

Jack Evans and Peter Drake were unboxing a

shipment of phonographs. Flora took two of the new items and arranged them artfully in the window with the three display radios. She placed the Edison model on one side of the window and the RCA model on the other. She placed several examples of records in the window, both the older cylinder records and the newer disc records.

A rather elderly couple came into the store. "We bought a radio here last week, but we don't know how to set it up," said the woman.

"Which model did you buy?" asked Flora who had finished her window display.

"We bought the four tube Radiola III.," said the man.

Jack Evans overheard the conversation and came over to the counter. "That is a good radio," Jack told them. "But it takes some training to use properly. What type of aerial are you using?"

"We put a wire in our window," explained the man.

"I think you need a long wire outside your house. I can come over and show you how to use the radio and string a long-wire antenna for you."

"How much do you charge for that?"

Jack looked at Peter for the answer. "We charge a dollar for installation, and it is well worth it." The man paid a dollar and gave Jack their address. They left the shop happy customers.

"Jack," said Peter, "I think you have a new task, radio installation.

"With that, plus radio repair, plus ordering phonographs, I think I can keep busy."

Flora Miller decided that she liked Jack's work ethic.

Both Bushy and Izzy were alarmed at the hysterical performance of Mary Brocton. She continued to laugh out of control. Bushy produced a syringe of some type of liquid and gave Mary a shot. She immediately quieted down.

"What on earth…" asked Izzy in an unfinished sentence.

"Something traumatic must have happened to her," Bushy had only seen this type of behavior in the asylum.

"What are we going to do?" Izzy asked. She was badly shaken by the event.

"I'm not sure," he replied. "I need to research this behavior further. When she comes around, you'll need to drive her home. And make sure she comes in tomorrow."

Isadora, Bushy, Peter and Flora sat in a corner of the New Meadows Inn. "Have you set a date?" she asked her brother.

"We thought we'd take our time. But someday when we are both ready we are going to elope."

"That sounds like a good idea," agreed Bushy. It would, after all, free him from helping his sister plan the wedding.

"Why Andrew Miller! I haven't seen you since

high school." The woman who stood in front of their table was of medium height, had a well-groomed bobbed hair style, and was wearing a fashionable dress, and white fur stole.

"Andrew?" Izzy never gave a thought to his real name. He had always been Bushy to her.

"Marie Westly, how are you? Have a seat," said Bushy as he got up to push in her chair.

"Marie and I went to high school together," explained Bushy.

"We did more than that," she announced to the table. Bushy's face suddenly turned beet red."

"How fortunate," quipped Izzy. She was enjoying seeing Bushy turn red. "Aren't you rather hot with those dead animals around your neck?"

"Marie, these are my friends," Bushy said quickly and went on to introduce her to the others.

"It gets so chilly at night," said Marie wrapping herself deeper in her stole. "I need a man to keep me warm all night." She put her hand on Bushy's arm and began to rub it.

Bushy moved in such a way that she had to let go of his arm. "You look wonderful," he told Marie.

This is war, Isadora told herself. "Yes, it's wonderful what lots and lots of makeup can do."

"Why I hardly have to use more than a little powder," she gave Izzy a murderous look.

"I like your lipstick and eyelashes," Flora took up the attack. "And the rouge looks almost natural."

"Aren't you a sweet little thing," and Marie shot her the same killer looks that Izzy had received. She looked at Bushy, "And I swear you get better looking with age."

"That's probably because he's younger than you," said Izzy with a sweat smile.

"Well, I better get going," said Marie. "I have a date." She stood up and the men stood. She hugged Bushy and kissed him on the cheek. Then she passed him a slip of paper. "It was interesting meeting you all." And she flounced out of the inn.

"I don't like her," Flora announced once the woman was out of sight.

"Nor do I," added Bushy. "I never liked her even in high school."

"What's on the paper?" asked Izzy.

"Let me see," Bushy opened the paper and read the note. "Hilltop Hotel room 36." He took the note and tore it into pieces and disposed of them in the ashtray.

The diner booth was crowded as Isadora joined the others for breakfast. Billy Brown, Jeff Starkey, and Anna Gray were already on the second cup of coffee as Izzy slid in beside Anna. "Sorry I'm late," she explained. "I had a hard time finding something to wear."

"I see you do have some clothes on," observed Jeff.

"It looks like you want to impress someone at the office," added Billy.

"I wonder who it could be," said Anna looking up at the ceiling.

"Droll, very droll," Izzy shot back.

"And how is that romance going?" asked Billy. "Have you two done the deed?"

"For your information, William, I'm a lady."

"That's not an answer," Jeff pointed out.

"How about non-of-your business," said Izzy trying hard to look offended.

"She hasn't," Anna answered the question.

"What's up with you two?" Isadora pointed to the two men.

"We're thinking of moving to New York where no one knows us and no one cares," answered Jeff.

"What about the house you want to build?" asked Izzy.

"That's all very nice," said Billy, "but we'd still be in Bath, wouldn't we?"

"You have a point," Anna agreed.

They ordered breakfast, and got caught up on local gossip. Just before Izzy left to go to the office Jeff told her to come to the police station at noon, and he would show her the suicide letter.

Chapter 25

As usual Flora Miller had the coffee ready by the time Isadora entered the office. She liked to talk to Izzy before she had to go off to Drake Radio. "How's your house guest doing?" Izzy asked Flora and their good morning greetings.

"He's very quiet and he cooked dinner for us last night."

"Billy can cook?" Isadora would never have guessed that a man could cook.

"Yes, and cook very well. We might keep him around. He says that cooking is the least he can do to thank us for taking him in."

"His father is an ass," swore Isadora.

"I don't doubt it, and his mother isn't any better."

"What are you two gossiping about?" asked Bushy when he came in from the kitchen.

"You and your fancy woman Marie," jeered Izzy.

"She's not my fancy woman," said Bushy.

"She's not done with you yet," replied Izzy. "I predict she'll show up here with a made-up health problem."

"Knock it off you two," warned Flora. "Mrs. Welby will be here anytime now." As if being summoned Mrs. Welby came in from the outside door.

"Good morning everyone," she said as she headed for the coffee pot. "It's a beautiful day."

"We're socked in with fog," Flora pointed out.

"Yes, well that fog will burn off and reveal a beautiful summer day."

The phone rang and Isadora went to answer it. She listened and had to keep from laughing. When she hung up she couldn't keep a straight face."

"What's so funny?" he asked.

"That was a patient who wanted to make an appointment with, as she put it, Doctor Andrew. Want to guess her name?"

"Shit," he said and shocked everyone in the office. Bushy never swore. "What does she want?"

"She said," and Isadora lowered her voice to a whisper, "female problems."

"Good god!" he exclaimed and crossed himself.

"What's going on?" asked Mrs. Welby who felt left out.

Isadora filled her in on their late-night visitor. She might have added a little color to the story more than was needed. "And she left him a note with her hotel and room number on it."

"The cheek!" Nurse Welby was shocked at Marie's boldness. "Don't worry Dr. Miller. I'll take care of her. I worked with a gynecologist for ten years. Just tell her I'll be doing the exam. The nerve!"

At noon she presented herself at the police station and was sent to Sergeant Starkey's desk. "I'm not sure what you're looking for," he told her, "we've gone over it carefully." He got up, went to a file cabinet, and pulled out a folder. "The letter is in there," and he passed the file to her. She carefully opened the file and began to slowly look it over.

"Pass me a sheet of paper," she said.

"Here you go."

She took the blank sheet of paper, placed the suicide note on top of it and held them up to the light.

"Take a look," she told him as he, too, held it up to the light.

"The only thing I see is that the suicide note is smaller." Then he saw it.

"The top of the page," she explained, though he had figured it out by now, "has been cut off. That is where the date usually is found. The date has been cut off. This isn't his suicide note. This is the note from his first suicide attempt. Someone kept it to use to make it look like suicide. That's why it's in his handwriting."

"I hate to admit it," Jeff said reluctantly, "but you're on to something. But we still have to find a motive."

Isadora noticed that he used 'we.' "I'm working on it."

Mary Brocton was scheduled to see Dr. Miller at one o'clock and arrived exactly on time. She was wearing, as Isadora described, a dress that was nun-like. Around her neck she had a very large crucifix. There was something off about the way she looked. Her expression was one of amusement, which wasn't like Mary at all.

"Good morning everyone," she said once she entered the office. "You look a little pale today Izzy."

"What?" Izzy was surprised at such a comment from Mary.

"I'm here to see that handsome doctor. I'd give him a toss."

"What?" asked Nurse Welby who was shocked by Mary's bold statement.

"What's wrong with you, Mary?" asked Izzy.

"What do you mean?" Mary asked.

"You just offered to give Dr. Miller, as you put it, a toss."

"I didn't say anything like that," she responded and then burst into tears.

"What's going on?" asked Bushy coming out of his office.

"I think Mary's having some sort of breakdown," Nurse Welby concluded.

"Bring her in and both of you stay with me in the exam room. Mrs. Welby, have a syringe of laudanum ready.”

"What's happening to me?" Mary wailed. "People keep saying that I say things that I don't say."

"There, there, calm down," Nurse Welby spoke in a soothing voice. "You're among friends." Bushy took advantage of the situation and gave Mary a shot of laudanum. Mary soon quieted down."

"Call the hospital," Bushy told Mrs. Welby, "and tell them we're bringing in a patient."

Chapter 26

Isadora Drake stood on the front steps of the yellow painted church, took a deep breath and climbed the stairs and entered the building. As a puritan descendent she was used to the plain New England protestant churches. This was something very different with its ornate stained glass, candles and statues.

Down the church's main aisle, she saw the figure of Father McKinney. He heard her entered and turned around. "Ah, the young lady with the injured ankle. How are you Miss Drake?"

"You have a good memory Father McKinney."

"It's my job. Have you decided to see the light and wish to become catholic?" he joked.

"I've come to ask you about Mary Brocton."

"I was under the impression she has been cleared as a suspect."

"I'm here about another matter concerning Mary."

"I see. We better go to my office and have a talk." He took her to the front of the church and through a side door to the church office. "Have a seat. You know I can't tell you anything she has said in confidence."

"But I'm not bound by such a restriction, so I'll share what I know and you can react or not to what I'm about to say."

"Very well, that sounds fair."

Isadora related how she and Anna had seen Mary at the Speak dressed in a gold dress and how she left on the arm of a married man. She explained that when she confronted Mary about her behavior, she denied it, and how when Isadora went to her closet and found the gold dress, she acted like she had never seen it before and swore someone was setting her up. "And I believe she was really confused and frighten," Isadora added.

"That's very peculiar," said the priest. Isadora added the latest scene in the doctor's office.

"She's at the hospital now. Have you noticed anything strange?"

"That's interesting about the clothing," the priest said thoughtfully. "One day at mass she came in all dressed up with makeup. Normally she's very modest in her dress. And I thought I heard her giggling during the service. What does all this mean?"

"Dr. Miller is trying to find out, but I was hoping you could help us."

"I'll go over to the hospital right now. And if I have any insight into the problem, I'll let Dr. Miller know. It's very good of you to share your concern."

"I just hope we can find out what's happening to her."

Isadora stood outside the office of Chamberlain and Brackett trying to think up a plan. She thought that maybe the answer to the Chamberlain murder might be inside, but she knew she couldn't just go inside and ask the workers if any of them had murdered Mr. Chamberlain. Well, she thought to herself, standing out here isn't going to help any.

"May I help you?" asked the receptionist at the front desk. Isadora was surprised at the woman's dress. It was bright red with green trim. Isadora thought it made her look like a skinny Christmas tree.

"I'm interested in getting a job," she answered. "I was wondering if there were any openings."

"As a matter of fact, we've had a death in the company, and we need a temporary file clerk to go through and organize the files that our late boss kept in his office. If you work out there may be a permanent position. You'll need to see Mrs. Milbourn the office manager. I'll take you to her."

Isadora was beside herself with glee. This had turned out better than she could have dreamed. Once Mrs. Milbourn learned that Isadora was a college graduate she was hired on the spot. Isadora would have to tell Bushy she would need a few days off.

At breakfast the next morning Rose Garland looked at Isadora with disbelief. "You got yourself another job?"

"It's part of my investigation." Izzy didn't want to say much more about the situation. She knew her grandmother and her friends liked a good gossip session.

"Don't you like being with Bushy every day?" asked Peter as he finished his breakfast.

"As I said this is part of an investigation, and it's only temporary."

"Well, it better be," grunted Peter. "Flora has to work the reception area of Bushy's office while you're doing god knows what at this temporary job."

"You can do without Flora for a day or two. You've got Jack Evans to help you out. Well, it's been a nice chat with you all, but I have to get to my new job."

Isadora reported to the Chamberlain and Brackett offices to start her new job. Mrs. Milbourn gave Isadora her list of duties, the first of which was to clean out Chamberlain's office. "You can start by filing all those reports on his desk," she told Isadora. "The new file folders are over here in the bottom drawer. Anything you find that you can't figure out come and see me."

"I understand."

"Very good. Do your best."

"I'm Mr. Brackett," said a man who poked his head into the office. "If you find anything that looks like a financial report bring it to my office.

I'm the third door on the left down the hall."

"I will, Mr. Brackett," she answered. "Like hell," she whispered after he left. Most of what she found were carbon copies of correspondences, letters to stockholders, and reports from major companies. She was able to create new files and file items in existing files in the file cabinets.

About an hour later Mr. Brackett poked his head into the office again. "Find anything?" he asked.

"Most of what I've filed so far are letters to clients and companies. Nothing that looks like a financial report."

"As I said, if you find any bring them to me immediately."

"Yes, sir, I will."

Isadora thought he was too eager to get his hands on some reports. He must have a good reason for it. She left the filings for the time being and began to look around the office. "So there must be something around here that he seems determined to get his hands on." In the corner of the room was a steel cabinet with a door that she saw had a lock. She headed over to exam the cabinet and found it unlocked. Inside all she saw were office supplies. She had already looked through the filing cabinets when she was filing and there was nothing of interest there.

"Find what you were looking for?" asked Mrs. Milbourn as Isadora was looking through the cabinet.

"I needed some paperclips," she said thinking quickly.

"Well, it's lunchtime so you need to go have your lunch."

Isadora headed over to her brother's store to have lunch. Flora had offered to make lunch for the crew. There was a small kitchen in the back of the store and, truth to tell, Flora loved to cook. The three radio workers, plus Bushy and Isadora, would break for lunch on most working days.

"What's new?" asked Bushy as he grabbed a sandwich and a cup of coffee.

"I'm buying the building," answered Peter. "There's an apartment upstairs where Flora and I will live after we are married."

"Are you sure you want to take him on?" Isadora asked Flora.

"You know, Flora," said Jack Evans as he grabbed another sandwich, "You should open a lunch counter. Food this good would make a lot of money."

"You think so?" asked Flora.

"Peter owns the building," added Bushy, "and that small space next door is empty."

"You'll have two incomes and you won't have to pay rent," observed Izzy.

"Actually, very practical," agreed Peter.

The phone rang and Jack went out to the front of the store and answered it. "That was for you Dr. Miller. You are needed at the office."

"I'll go, too," offered Flora, "so your nurse can go to lunch."

"And I should get back to the office since it's my first day on the job," said Izzy as she gathered up her things.

"How was lunch?" asked Mrs. Milbourn as Isadora entered the office.

"It was very nice, thank you. I should get back to work." Isadora entered the office and continued to file away documents until she was sure that everyone else was busy and she would be undisturbed. It was time to examine Chamberlain's desk. The top drawer held pens and pencils and a spare box of staples. Two more drawers proved the same. Nothing significant. When she tried the fourth drawer, she found that it was locked. "That's interesting," she said to herself.

Taking out a nail file from her purse she tried to jimmy open the lock, but it wouldn't budge. "Where would he hide the key." She felt under the desk and found a piece of tape that was holding not one key, but two. "What the heck?"

She pulled them out and laid them side by side. There were not the same. One of them was smaller and probably made for the desk, but what in the world did the second key go to?

She took the smaller key and tried it in the locked desk drawer and it fit. She turned the lock and slowly opened the drawer. Inside she saw an appointment book. She thought for sure the police had gone through the office, but as she thought about it she realized that suicide probably involved a simple investigation since it wasn't a crime involving anyone else.

Inside the drawer she was shocked to find a

gun. This wasn't the gun he was shot with and if this was suicide why didn't he shoot himself with this gun? Why have two guns? She picked up the phone and called the police station and asked to speak with sergeant Starkey.

"I have something interesting to report. I'll be in your office around five after I get out of work."

"Can't you tell me over the phone?"

"I'd rather not. See you soon," she said and hung up the phone.

Dr. Bushy Miller had done some more research and was beginning to have some ideas about what was happening to Mary Brocton. He began making phone calls and set up an appointment with Mary for the next evening. Was someone setting her up or... he wasn't sure, but maybe there was a simple explanation.

Jeff Starkey heard Isadora's footsteps coming down the hall before she appeared. "Nice shoes," he said as a greeting.

"They are about as nice as your tie," she countered. "You shouldn't wear red."

"Have a seat and tell me what you are so secretive about."

"I managed to get a job at Chamberlain and Brackett and they hired me to clean up some of the files in Chamberlain's office."

"Still on that merry-go-round are you? Trying to prove Chamberlain was murdered?"

"Are you going to listen or not?" she had a date with Bushy and wanted to get home and change.

"Fine, go ahead," he sighed.

"Where is the gun with which Chamberlain shot himself?"

"We have it here in evidence."

"Who found the body?"

"Mrs. Milbourn, why?"

"Who else was in the building when she discovered the body?"

"No one it was early morning before the office opened. What is this all about?"

"When I opened a locked desk drawer of Chamberlain's desk I found a gun. Why would he have another gun when he already had one handy in his desk?"

Jeff was speechless for a moment. "A gun?"

"Yes, you know one of those metal things that shoots bullets? You might want to get a search warrant and check for yourself." She reached into her handbag and pulled out the key and set it in front of him. "Now if you will excuse me, I have to get ready for a date." She picked up the keys and deposited them in her purse.

Bushy arrived at Isadora's house to pick her up. Rose answered the door. "She'll be down shortly," Rose informed him.

"That's fine," he answered. "I enjoy spending time with you."

"Flattery," she told him, "gets you a few points. Here she is now."

Bushy turned around and saw Isadora dressed in a light green dress that brought out her green eyes. It was as if he was seeing her for the first time. "You look wonderful."

"And you look handsome," she noticed that he was wearing a new pinstripe suit.

"Let me get my camera," said Rose. "You make a great couple."

Chapter 27

As Bushy and Isadora entered the crowded Bath Opera House, they were able to find two seats together where they could snuggle in the dark. The organ music began playing and the house lights started to dim. The first movie was the short film The Boat, with Buster Keaton followed by the film The Four Horsemen of the Apocalypse. Isadora watched with fascination as Rudolf Valentino and Alice Terry danced the tango across the screen. Bushy, however, found the film disturbing. It had only been three years since the Great War, and it brought back memories of all the men at college whose lives were interrupted by enlisting. Some came back, but two of his good friends had not returned.

When the movie was over, they walked over to the Speak in silence. Each processing the images from the movie. The Speak was noisy and smoke filled. They found a table where they could look around at the crowd. "What did you think of the flicker?" Bushy asked as they sat down. He signaled the waiter and two beers appeared on the table.

"It's amazing how you can be transported into a different place and time."

"That's what I was thinking. I got totally lost in the story."

"It was rather an anti-war film," added Isadora. "It did not glorify the war."

A couple entered the bar and stood at the top of the stairs and looked around at the partiers in the subterranean speakeasy. "Isn't that..." Bushy said.

"Yes, that's Mary Brocton and some man with her,"

"But she should be in the hospital," protested Bushy.

"Well, she's not is she?" Izzy commented.

"I'm going to go over there and send her back." He began to stand up.

"Sit down, Bushy. This will be a good opportunity to watch and see how she behaves."

"Look at how she's dressed," observed Bushy.

"I'm going to guess that she's missing her undergarments."

"She sees us," said Bushy. "She's coming over."

Mary left her date and came over to their table and sat down in the empty chair. "Well, if it isn't goody, goody Isadora and the sexy doctor. I'll bet she hasn't given you what you need. I could just slip my hand under the table and make your day."

This was too much for Izzy and she got up and took Mary by the shoulders and started shaking her. "What is wrong with you?" she yelled as people turned to watch the proceedings. Mary slumped in the chair for a moment and then looked confused. "Izzy? What am I doing here? Where are we?" and she burst into tears.

Sergeant Starkey entered the office of Chamberlain and Brackett and asked to see Mr. Chamberlain's office and produced a search warrant. Mrs. Milbourn looked surprised, but told him where the office was. "We have a girl in there filing now," she said.

"I'll be nice," he said. He knew Isadora was no girl and would probably object to the term. "Good morning, Izzy," he said and closed the door as he entered.

"That's the drawer there," she pointed to the desk. He took out the key that she had given him and opened the drawer. He carefully picked up the gun with a handkerchief to avoid putting finger prints on it and slipped it into his pocket.

"Anything else you observed while you were here?" he asked her.

"Mr. Brackett keeps asking me if I've come across any financial records."

"That's interesting. Anything else?"

"I found two keys. That one goes to the drawer, and I've no idea what the second one goes to," she told him.

"It looks like some type of strong box key."

"How can you tell?"

"Because I'm a real detective," he said laughing.

"I hope you are not laughing at me," she scowled. "I've looked everywhere for something that the key would open."

He looked around. "Did you look behind that painting?"

"No, why?"

"That's usually where they install lock boxes and safes." He went over to the painting and moved it aside. Behind the painting was a steel lockbox built into the wall. "Do you still have the key?"

"Yes, it's in my purse." She opened up her purse, fished around and handed the key to him. He carefully inserted the key and opened the door. Inside was a ledger book.

"This looks interesting," he said as he took the book out and opened it.

"What's in it?" she asked him.

"I'm not sure. I don't know much about bookkeeping. I'll take it to the station and have someone who knows accounting look at it."

Dr. Bushy Miller's office was crowded because he had called everyone in who he thought was involved in Mary Brocton's life. Izzy, Anna Gray, and Billy were there, as were her parents and Father McKinney, the priest.

"I've asked you all to come here to discuss Mary's recent behavior," announced Bushy when they had all assembled.

"What do you mean her behavior?" asked Mrs. Brocton.

"Haven't you noticed anything unusual about her behavior?" Bushy asked the mother.

"Well," she admitted, "she's been keeping to herself. She goes upstairs early, and we don't see her until late morning when she gets up."

"Mr. Brocton?" Bushy turned to the father.

"She has been a little rebellious lately. She's been contradicting me. That's not like her."

"Miss Gray," Bushy turned to her. "When did you last see her?"

"I saw her last week at the speakeasy. She was dressed provocatively in a gold dress, had on lots of makeup, and was keeping company with a married man."

"That's impossible," stated the mother in anger.

"I'm afraid it's true," added Isadora. "We talked to her and we know for a fact that it was she."

"Isadora and I also saw her at the Speak on another occasion," Bushy told them.

"And she said some very improper suggestions to Dr. Miller," Izzy added.

"Like what?" demanded her father.

"She offered," said Isadora, "To slip her hand under the table and give Dr Miller a thrill." She wasn't completely clear on what that meant but Izzy had a good idea.

There was shocked silence for a few moments. "During mass," added Father McKinney, "twice lately at a weekday mass she has burst out giggling."

"So," concluded Dr. Miller, "I think she needs more help than we can give her."

"You want to put her into an insane asylum?"

"No, I don't," Bushy said quickly. "Asylums are really just warehousing for the insane. No, I've found a private clinic where I think she can get some help. It's well thought of in the medical community." Bushy gave the parents the business card of the clinic. "Of course, it's your call. But I believe she's headed for a complete breakdown."

"Thank you," said the parents in a low-key manner as they took the business card from Bushy and headed out the door.

"You should really thank Miss Drake," said Bushy. "She's the one who brought this to my attention."

"And mine, too," added Father McKinney.

Chapter 28

Despite the fact that they were all crowded into Bushy Miller's Model T Ford, it was a pleasant ride to Freeport. Following them was Peter Drake's new 1921 Owen-Magnetic touring car. It was nice to get out of town for a break. The weather was one of those late summer days when the sun was warm and the breeze was cool. Heading to the Stage Coach Inn they parked their automobiles on the side of the road and entered the old inn. Inside the dining room was decorated with colonial furniture including an old spinning wheel next to a huge colonial hearth. Once inside they were shown to a large table near an open window where they could enjoy the view and the fresh breeze.

It was a large table for the four couples; Bushy and Isadora, Billy Brown and Jeff Starkey, Peter Drake and Flora Miller, and Anna Gray and her steady beau Michael Frazer.

"I don't suppose we can get a drink here," sighed Anna.

"Freeport is a dry town," reported Izzy.

"Since when?" asked Michael.

"Since prohibition, you big dummy," said Anna with affection.

"What's going to happen to Mary Brocton?" Billy asked Bushy.

"She suffered some type of mental breakdown," answered Bushy. "One part of her rebelled against being a good girl, so part of her became a bad girl. She doesn't realize yet what is going on. I hope they can help her at the clinic, but I think it's going to be a long time before she can return."

"And you weren't tempted by her offers?" asked Michael. Anna gave him a slap on the arm.

"My temptation is elsewhere," Bushy looked straight at Izzy, who blushed bright red.

"Ready to order?" asked the waiter, who interrupted their conversation. They gave their orders and watched him walk away. Billy and Jeff seemed more intent on the waiter.

"When are you two moving?" asked Bushy.

"We're not," answered Jeff. "Let people think what they want. I'm buying a farm house in North Bath far from prying eyes where we can be ourselves."

"I heard the murder case has been reopened," Billy commented on, more to change the subject than out of interest.

"So far Izzy has uncovered some interesting facts," explained Jeff. "But nothing yet that helps us find a motive or a killer."

"Not yet anyway," added Izzy. "I'm working on it. By the way, getting back to Mary Brocton, what was this hand thing she was talking about?" There was a shocked silence and then everyone burst out in hysterical laughter.

"Oh, Izzy!" said Anna. "You are too much!"

"Why? What did I say?"

Anna whispered in Izzy's ear.

"Oh, oh! That's a real thing?"

"I don't get it either," admitted Flora.

"I'll explain it to you later," promised Anna.

Feeling both foolish and uncomfortable Izzy changed the subject. "Jeff what did the police find out about the records we found in Chamberlain's office?"

"There is something about the records that make no sense, but we don't know what it is. We've asked an accountant to come in and have a look. It's beyond our bookkeeper's knowledge."

"Are you going back to work there?" asked Bushy.

"For a few more days just to see if I can get more information."

"Here comes the food," said Billy.

"I'm starving," Peter said. "Let's eat."

Isadora Drake presented herself at the office the next morning where she was greeted by Mrs. Melbourne. "Good morning Miss Drake. Have a seat,"

Isadora took a seat and waited for her to speak. "I'll get right to the point. We have been pleased with your work and would like to offer you the job."

"Thank you. I'd like that," Izzy lied.

"The next thing we'd like you to do is to find a missing financial report. It will be inside a cover that looks like this." She held up a report with a blue cover. Isadora recognized the cover because it was the same color as the one she gave to Sergeant Starkey. "When you find it bring it to me or to Mr. Brackett. It's very important that we find it."

"I'll do my best," she promised. "Do you know where he would keep it?"

"No, it's not something he would normally have. He seems to have taken it from Mr. Brackett's office." This was interesting information. She would tell Jeff Starkey at lunch. She picked up the phone and dialed Jeff at the police station.

Sergeant Jeff Starkey and Isadora Drake were at the Kennebec Diner having lunch. "Believe it or not they want to hire me full time," Isadora was telling Jeff what she found out and what she had figured out. I think they offered me the job to keep me quiet in case I found out anything looking through the files."

"Well, as a matter of fact I have some news. The accountant found that there were, as we suspected, some irregularities in the bookkeeping."

"Irregularities?"

"It seems," Jeff informed her, "that both Mr. Brackett and Mrs. Melbourne have been dipping into the profits."

"Which, I guess, is why they were both so interested in finding the file," added Isadora. "So here is what I think happened. Mr. Chamberlain found the file in Mr. Brackett's office. He must have been suspicious that something was off to search for the file. He must have taken it and hidden it in his lock box. Being a businessman, he knew how to interpret the financial records. He probably confronted them and threatened to file embezzlement charges. Somehow, I don't know how, but one of them remembered that he had tried to commit suicide in the past and they got hold the old suicide note. They cut off the top of the note where the date was, shot him, put the gun in his hand, and the suicide note on his desk. What they didn't realize was that Mr. Chamberlain had a gun hidden in the back of the desk drawer. So then the question was why didn't he shoot himself with his own gun.? That was their first mistake."

"And the second mistake was letting you into their business," said Jeff with admiration. "As much as it grieves me to say this, you are a good detective. And if you hadn't taken on this case two murderers would be getting away with murder. And your reward will be getting to see me arrest the two of them for murder."

"And can you make it stick. It's mostly conjecture and circumstantial."

"There are two of them, one of them will confess in order to get a reduced sentence. Murderers usually try to save their own necks and give up their partners."

Isadora was working quietly in the office with the door open when she saw Sergeant Starkey and two uniformed officers enter the outer office. "Get Mr. Brackett in here," he said to Mrs. Melbourne.

"I'll see if he's available," she said and picked up the phone.

"Never mind," he said. "I'll drag him out here myself." Jeff came out dragging a very reluctant Mr. Brackett.

"What's the meaning of this?" asked Brackett. Isadora had noticed the color had drained from Mrs. Melbourne's face.

"I'm arresting you both for the murder of Jasper Chamberlain. "Cuff them," he said to the two policemen.

"It was all his idea!" screamed Mrs. Melbourne.

"Shut up you old cow!" Mr. Brackett screamed back at her.

"Get them out of here," the sergeant told the two officers, "and book them."

"I think, my dear," Jeff said to Izzy, "that we deserve a drink down at the Speak."

"I think you might be right."

It didn't take long for the news of the arrest to take place. *The Bath Independent* reported the news in its next edition, and a day later Isadora received a check from the Wickers for a substantial amount. The police department had issued a news release that a citizen, Isadora Drake, had aided the police. What surprised Isadora was the reaction of the town. Everywhere she went citizens greeted her by name. It was that Bath was a small city, but still. In fact, she had received two requests for her services, and it was beginning to look like she would be able to make, as she put it, some pin money.

Summer in Maine is all too brief. One day you have the windows open hoping for a breeze, and the next morning when you wake up you need to start a fire. The payoff for the short summers is the autumn when the trees begin to show their vibrant colors and the sky is the bluest it has ever been. It was on such a day that her brother Peter was to marry Flora Miller.

Rose Garland had offered her house for the service. As far as anyone knew, there hadn't been a wedding in the house since 1865 when the original owner of the house returned from the Civil War. The Gothic Revival house still looked very much as it had in the past. True, the gas lights had been converted to electricity, and modern plumbing had been added, but for all its updates, it was still like stepping back in time.

Flora, Izzy, Anna and Billy had been working on the apartment over the store where the newlyweds would live, though they planned to build a house someday. They had painted the walls, and bought furniture, and surprisingly, or maybe not, Billy turned out to be a good decorator. He arranged the furniture, helped the ladies choose the paintings, put up the drapes, and added the little touches.

"I think you've found what you are good at," Izzy told him.

"You should start a business," added Flora. "You've done a wonderful job. I couldn't do nearly half as good as you have.

"You think so?" he asked somewhat surprised.

"Yes, I think so," added Anna.

It was supposed to be a small gathering, but word had spread and it seemed the whole town showed up. Bushy was Peter's Best man, and Isadora would be Flora's Maid of Honor. The Millers had returned to Bath to attend the wedding. Mr. Miller would give his daughter away. And after the ceremony there would be a reception at the New Meadows Inn.

The wedding was delayed because the minister was late, but when he finally showed up the wedding got underway. As Flora and Izzy descended the stairs there was an audible gasp. Flora, with her hair covered by a vail, seemed to float like an angel. The white dress looked like gossamer and Peter was speechless. Bushy, too, was speechless as he looked at Isadora dressed in a formal gown of lavender. The service was short which was just as the couple planned, and everyone left for the reception at the inn.

Near the bride and groom's table, the "bright young things" were seated together.

"Well here we are again," said Anna. "Hopefully there won't be a murder this time."

"Just think how much things have changed since then," said Billy.

"It was an unusual summer," said Jeff.

"Did Billy tell you about his new career?" Izzy asked Jeff.

"He did and I think it's a great idea."

"And what about you?" Bushy asked Isadora. "Are you going to work for me or are you going to be a detective."

"I'm going to do both. I love working for you and I love solving mysteries."

The conversation stopped as the band began playing and the newlyweds danced. Once the couple finished the dance others got up to dance.

Bushy took Isadora by the hand and they headed to the dance floor. As they danced Bushy whispered in her ear.

"Did the wedding put any ideas in your head?"

She looked up at him. "I have plenty of ideas. Not all of which are decent."

"Are you opposed to long engagements?"

"I like the idea. Are you proposing?"

"I guess I am," he said surprising himself.

"Well, I'll have to think it over,"

"Of course."

In about thirty seconds she replied, "I've thought it over and the answer is yes. But let's keep it a secret for a while. I don't want to compete with Peter and Flora's big day. Flora is now my sister-in -law."

"And I'm Peter's brother-in-law."

"And as soon as the couple departs for their honeymoon," she suggested, "let's slip away."

"My thoughts exactly."

The end

9 798869 826056 1